"Bernadette," he whispered in a tone she'd never heard him use before. She was frozen in time, in space. She wanted his mouth to come down and cover hers. She wanted to taste it, and she'd wanted to so often in the past two years, even as she feared the change that it would bring to their turbulent relationship. But at the moment, the blood was surging through her veins and she was hungry for something she'd never known. The lack of restraint made her reckless.

Involuntarily, she leaned closer to him, her lips approaching his as she forgot all her upbringing in the heat of sudden desire. . . .

By Diana Palmer
Published by Fawcett/Ivy Books:

LACY
TRILBY
AMELIA
NORA
NOELLE
MAGNOLIA
THE SAVAGE HEART
MIDNIGHT RIDER

MIDNIGHT RIDER

Diana Palmer

FAWCETT GOLD BOOKS • NEW YORK

A Fawcett Gold Book
Published by The Ballantine Publishing Group
 Published in the United States by The Ballantine Publishing Group, a division of Random House, Inc., New York, and simultaneously in Canada by Random House of Canada Limited, Toronto.

http://www.randomhouse.com

Library of Congress Catalog Card Number: 98-96397

ISBN 0-449-00324-8

Manufactured in the United States of America

First Edition: October 1998

10 9 8 7 6 5 4 3 2 1

Chapter One

Southwestern Texas, 1900

IN ALL THE WORLD THERE WAS NOTHING BERNADETTE Barron loved more than her garden, despite the asthma that sometimes sent her running from it in the spring months. There were plenty of flowers in southwestern Texas, and many occasions to fill her father's elaborate Victorian home with them. Colston Barron owned at least half of Valladolid County, which was midway between the prosperous city of San Antonio and the smaller city of Del Rio on the Mexican border.

He had done extremely well for an Irish immigrant who got his start working on building the railroads. Now, thirty-three years after his arrival in the United States, he owned two. He had money to burn, but little family to spend it on.

Despite his wealth, there was one thing still lacking in his life—acceptance and respect from elite society. His rude Irish brogue and lack of conventional manners isolated him from the prominent families of the day, a situation he was determined to change. And Bernadette was going to be the means of it.

His beloved wife, Eloise, had died of an infection just after giving birth to Bernadette. His eldest daughter had died in childbirth. His only son, married with a small child, lived back East, worked as a fisherman, and kept contact with his father to a minimum. Albert was in disgrace because he'd married for love, refusing the social match his father had planned for him. Only Bernadette was left at home now. Her brother could barely support his own small family, so running to him was not an option unless she was able to work, which was impossible because her health was too precarious to allow her to hold down a job, such as teaching. Meanwhile, she had to cope with her father's fanatical social aspirations.

It wasn't that Bernadette didn't want to marry, eventually. She had her own dreams of a home and family. But her father wanted to choose her husband—on the basis of his social prominence. Wealth alone would not do. Colston Barron was determined to marry off Bernadette to a man with a title or, if he were an American, to a man of immense social prestige. His first choice, a British duke, had been a total loss. The impoverished nobleman was willing enough. Then he was introduced to Bernadette, who had appeared at the first meeting, for reasons known only to herself and

God, in her brother's tattered jeans, a dirty shirt, with two of her teeth blackened with wax and her long, beautiful platinum hair smeared with what looked like axle grease. The duke had left immediately, excusing himself with the sudden news of an impending death in the family. Although how he could have known of it in this isolated region of southwest Texas . . .

All Colston's mad raving hadn't made Bernadette repent. She was not, she informed him saucily, marrying any man for a title! Her brother had left some of his old clothes at the ranch and Bernadette wasn't a bit averse to dressing like a madwoman anytime her father brought a marriage prospect home. Today, though, she was off her guard. In a blue-checked dress with her platinum blond hair in its familiar loose bun and her green eyes soft with affection for the roses she was tending, she didn't seem a virago at all. Not to the man watching her unseen from his elegant black stallion.

All at once she felt as if she were being watched . . . scrutinized . . . by a pair of fierce, dark eyes. His eyes, of course. Amazing, she thought, how she always seemed to sense him, no matter how quietly he came upon her.

She got to her feet and turned, her high cheekbones flushed, her pale green eyes glittering at the elegant black-clad man in his working clothes—jeans and boots and chaps, a chambray shirt under a denim jacket, his straight black hair barely visible under a wide-brimmed hat that shadowed his face from the hot sun.

"Shall I curtsey, your excellence?" she asked, throwing down the gauntlet with a wicked smile. There was always a slight antagonism between them.

Eduardo Rodrigo Ramirez y Cortes gave her a mocking nod of his head and a smile from his thin, cruel-looking mouth. He was as handsome as a dark angel, except for the slash down one cheek, allegedly garnered in a knife fight in his youth. He was thirty-six now, sharp-faced, olive-skinned, black-eyed, and dangerous.

His father, a titled Spanish nobleman, had been dead for many years. His mother, a beautiful blond San Antonio socialite, was in New York with her second husband. Eduardo had no more inherited his mother's looks than he had absorbed her behavior and temperament. He was in all ways Spanish. To the workers on his ranch he was El Jefe, the patron or boss. In Spain, he was El Conde, a count whose relatives could be found in all the royal families across Europe. To Bernadette, he was the enemy. Well, sometimes he was. She fought with him to make sure that he didn't realize what she really felt for him—emotions that had been harder these past two years to conceal than ever.

"If you're looking for my father, he's busy

thinking of rich San Antonio families to invite to his ball a month from next Saturday evening," she informed him, silently seething. From the shadow his brim made on his lean face, the black glitter of his eyes was just visible. He looked her over insolently for such a gentleman and then dismissively, as if he found nothing to interest him in her slender but rounded figure and small breasts. His late wife, she recalled, although a titled Spanish lady of high quality, had been nothing less than voluptuous. Bernadette had tried to gain weight so that she could appeal to him more, but her slender frame refused to add pounds despite her efforts.

"He has hopes of an alliance with a titled European family," Eduardo replied. "Have you?"

"I'd rather take poison," she said quietly. "I've already sent one potential suitor running for the border, but my father won't give up. He's planning a ball to celebrate his latest railroad acquisition—but more because he's found another two impoverished European noblemen to throw at my feet."

She took a deep breath and coughed helplessly until she was able to get her lungs under control. The pollen sometimes affected her. She hated showing her weakness to Eduardo.

He crossed his forearms over the pommel of his saddle and leaned forward. "A garden is hardly a good place for an asthmatic," he pointed out.

"I like flowers." She took a frilled, embroidered

handkerchief from her belt and held it to her mouth. Her eyes above it were green and hostile. "Why don't you go home and flog your serfs?" she retorted.

"I don't have serfs. Only loyal workers who tend my cattle and watch over my house." He ran a hand slowly over one powerful thigh while he studied her with unusual interest. "I thought your father had given up throwing you at every available titled man."

"He hasn't run out of candidates yet." She sighed and looked up at him with more of her concern showing than she realized. "Lucky you, not to be on the firing line."

"I beg your pardon?"

"Well, you're titled, aren't you?"

He laughed softly. "In a sense."

"You're a count, el conde," she persisted.

"I am. But your father knows that I have had no wish to marry since I lost my son. And my wife," he added bitterly.

"Well, it's reassuring that you don't want to get married again," she said.

She knew little of his tragedy except that for a space of days after it, the "ice man" had become a local legend for his rage, which was as majestic as his bloodlines. Grown men had hidden from him. On one occasion Bernadette had encountered him when he was dangerously intoxicated and wildly waving a revolver. . . . No one knew exactly what had happened, except that Eduardo had come home to find his infant son dead. His wife had died suddenly soon afterward of a gunshot wound to the head. No arrest had ever been made, no charges brought. Eduardo never spoke of what had happened, but inevitably there were whispers that he had blamed his wife for the child's death, and that he had killed her. Looking at him now she could almost believe him capable of murder. He was as hard a man as she'd ever known, and one she judged to be merciless when he had reason to become angry. He rarely lost his temper overtly, but his icy manner was somehow more threatening than yelling.

She herself had seen him shoot a man with cold nerve, a drunken cowboy in town who'd come at him with pistols blazing.

Eduardo hadn't even bothered to duck. He stood in a hail of bullets and calmly took aim and fired. The man went down, wounded but not dead, and he was left at the doctor's office. Eduardo had been nicked in the arm and refused Bernadette's offer of first aid. Such a scratch, he'd said calmly, was hardly worth a fuss.

She had hoped against hope that her father might one day consider making a match for her with this man. Eduardo was the very reason her heart beat. Just the thought of those hard, cool hands on her bare skin made her tingle all over. But an alliance between the families had never been discussed. Her father had looked only to Europe for her prospective bridegrooms, not closer to home.

"You have no wish to marry?" he asked suddenly.

The question caught her unaware. "I have bad lungs," she said. "And I'm not even pretty. My father has money, which makes me very eligible, but only to fortune-seekers." She twisted a fold of her skirt unconsciously in her slender, pretty hands. "I want to be worth more than that."

"You want to be loved."

Shock brought her eyes up. How had he known that? He did know. It was in his face.

"Love is a rare and often dangerous thing," he continued carelessly. "One does well to avoid it."

"I've been avoiding it successfully all my life," she agreed with smothered humor.

His eyes narrowed. Still watching her, he pulled a thin black cigar from a gold-plated case in his jacket. He replaced the case deftly, struck a match to light the cigar, and threw the spent match into the dust with careless grace. "All your life," he murmured. "Twenty years. You must have been ten when your family moved here," he added thoughtfully. "I remember your first ride on horseback."

She did, too. The horse had pitched her over its head into a mud puddle. Eduardo had found her there, dazed. Ignoring the mud that covered her front liberally, he'd taken her up in the saddle before him and delivered her to her father.

She nodded uncomfortably. "You were forever finding me in embarrassing situations." She didn't even want to remember the last one. . . .

"His name was Charles, wasn't it?" he asked, as if he'd read her mind, and he smiled mockingly.

She glared at him. "It could have happened to anyone! Buggy horses do run away, you know!"

"Yes. But that horse had the mark of a whip clearly on its flank. And the 'gentleman' in question had you flat on your back, struggling like a landed fish, and your dress—"

"Please!" She held a hand to her throat, horribly embarrassed.

His eyes went to her bodice with a smile that chilled her. He'd seen more than her corset. Charles had roughly exposed her small breasts from beneath her thin muslin chemise and Eduardo had had a vivid glimpse of them before she struggled to get them covered again. Charles had barely had time to speak before el conde was on him.

In a very rare display of rage, the usually calm and collected Eduardo had knocked the younger man around with an utter disregard for his family's great wealth until the son of the shipping magnate was bleeding and begging on his knees for mercy. He'd headed for town, walking fast, and he hadn't been seen again. Naturally, Bernadette's father had been given a very smoothed-over explanation for Charles's absence and her own ruffled state. He'd accepted it, even if he hadn't believed it. But it hadn't stopped him from throwing titled men at her.

"Your father is obsessed," Eduardo murmured, taking a puff from the cigar and letting it out angrily. "He puts you at risk."

"If I'd had my pistol, Mr. Charles Ramsey would have been lying on the ground with a bullet in him!"

He only smiled. To his knowledge, Bernadette couldn't even load a gun, much less shoot one. He smoked his cigar in silence as he studied her. "Did you ever hear from the unfortunate Charles again?" he asked abruptly.

"Not one word." She searched his hard, lean face and remembered graphically how it had looked when he hit Charles. "You were frightening."

"Surely not to you."

"You're so controlled most of the time," she said, underscoring the words "most of the time."

Something moved in his face, something indefinable. "Any man is capable of strong passion. Even me."

The way he was looking at her made her heart skip. Unwelcome thoughts came into her mind, only to be banished immediately. They were too disturbing to entertain. She looked away and asked, "Are you coming to the ball?"

"If I'm invited," he said easily.

Her eyebrows arched. "Why wouldn't you be? You're one of the upper class that my father so envies."

His laughter was cold. "Me? I'm a half-breed, don't you remember?" He shifted in the saddle. "My grandmother can't make a match for me in Spain because my wife died under mysterious circumstances and I'm staring poverty in the face. In my own way, I have as few opportunities for marriage as you do."

She hadn't thought of it that way. "You're titled."

"Of course," he conceded. "But only in Spain, and I have no plans to live there." He was looking at her, but now his mind was working on the problem of bankruptcy, which was staring him in the face. His late father had made a fortune, but his profligate mother had thrown it away. She had drained the financial resources of the ranch, and since he'd come of age Eduardo had been hard-pressed to keep it solvent. Only his mother's marriage to some minor millionaire in New York had stopped her from bleeding the ranch dry. She had forfeited her inheritance the day she remarried, but the damage already had been done.

Eduardo stared down at Bernadette and wheels turned in his mind. Her father was rich. He wanted a titled son-in-law. Eduardo was upper class, despite his mixed ancestry. Perhaps . . . Bernadette sighed heavily, smothering another cough. "At least you'll never have to worry about being married for your father's money."

"And this idea of marrying a title and a respected name has no appeal at all for you?" he asked slowly.

"None," she said honestly. She grimaced. "I'm so tired of being on display, like a bargain that my father's offering for sale!" she said, drawing in a long, labored breath. She coughed suddenly, aware of a renewed tightness in her chest. She hadn't realized how long she'd been among her flowers, with their potent quantities of pollen. "I have to go in," she said as the cough came again. "The flowers smell wonderful, but they bother my lungs when I spend too much time with them."

He scowled. "Then why are you out here?"

She coughed once again. "The house . . . my father has men repainting the ballroom. The paint bothers me."

"Then going inside the front of the house is hardly a solution, is it?"

She tried to clear her throat enough to answer him, but thick mucus was all but choking her.

Eduardo threw his cigar down and swung gracefully out of the saddle. Seconds later, he lifted her into his arms.

"Eduardo!" she cried, shocked at the unaccustomed familiarity, the strength and hard warmth of those arms around her. She could see his eyes far too closely, feel his warm breath at her temple, touch, if she wished, the hard, cruel curve of his beautiful mouth. . . .

"Calmarte," he murmured softly, searching her taut face. "I mean only to take you in through the kitchen to the conservatory. There are no blooming plants there to cause you discomfort." He shook her gently. "Put your arms around my neck, Bernadette. Don't lie like a log against me."

She shivered and obeyed him, secretly all but swooning at the pure joy of being so close to him. He smelled of leather and exotic cologne, a secret, intimate smell that wasn't noticeable at a distance. Oddly, it didn't disturb her lungs as some scents did.

She laid her cheek gingerly against his shoulder and closed her eyes with a tiny sigh that she hoped he wouldn't hear. It was all of heaven to be carried by him. She hadn't dreamed of such an unexpected pleasure coming to her out of the blue.

His strong, hard arms seemed to contract for an instant. Then, all too soon, they reached the kitchen. He put her down, opened the door, and coaxed her through it. Maria was in the kitchen making a chicken dish for the midday meal. She glanced up, flustered, to see their landed neighbor inside her own kitchen, with his hat respectfully in his hand.

"Señor Conde! What an honor!" Maria gasped.

"I am only Mr. Ramirez, Maria," he said with an affectionate smile.

She made a gesture. "You are el conde to me. My son continues to please you with his work, I hope?"

"Your son is a master with unbroken horses," he said in rare praise. "I am fortunate to have him at the rancho."

"He is equally fortunate to serve you, Señor Conde."

Obviously, Eduardo thought, he wasn't destined to have much luck in persuading Maria to stop using his title.

Bernadette tried to smile, but the cough came back, worse than ever.

"Ay, ay, ay," Maria said, shaking her head. "Again, it is the flowers, and I fuss and fuss but you will not listen!"

"Strong coffee, Maria, black and strong," Eduardo instructed. "You will bring it to the conservatory, yes? And then inform Señor Barron that I am here?"

"But of course! He is in the barn with a new foal, but he will return shortly."

"Then I will find him myself, once I have made Bernadette comfortable. I am pressed for time." He took Bernadette's arm and propelled her down the long, tiled hall to a sunny room where green plants, but no flowering ones, grew in profusion and a water garden flourished in its glassed-in confines.

She sat down with her face in her hands, struggling to breathe.

He muttered something and knelt before her, his hands capturing hers. "Breathe slowly, Bernadette. Slowly." His hands pressed hers firmly. "Try not to panic. It will pass, as it always does."

She tried, but it was an effort. Her tired eyes met his and she was surprised again at the concern there. How very odd that her enemy seemed at times like her best friend. And how much more odd that he seemed to know exactly what to do for her asthma. She said it aloud without thinking.

"Yes, we do fight sometimes, don't we?" he murmured, searching her face. "But the wounds always heal."

"Not all of them."

His eyebrows lifted.

"You say harsh things when you're angry," she reminded him, averting her eyes.

"And what have I said, most recently, that piques you?"

She shifted restlessly, unwilling to recall the blistering lecture she'd received from him after her unfortunate ride with Charles.

He tilted her face back to his. "Tell me."

"You can't remember?" she asked mutinously.

"I said that you had no judgment about men,"

he recalled. "And that it was just as well that . . ." His mouth closed abruptly.

"I see that you do remember," she muttered irritably, avoiding his dark, unblinking gaze.

"Bernadette," he began softly, pressing her hands more gently, and choosing his words very carefully, calculatingly, "didn't you realize that the words were more frustration than accusation? I barely arrived in time to save you from that lout, and I was upset."

"It was cruel."

"And untrue," he added. "Come on, look at me."

She did, still mutinous and resentful.

He leaned forward, his breath warm on her lips as he spoke. "I said it was just as well that you had money as you had so few attributes physically with which to tempt a man."

She started to speak, but his gloved finger pressed hard against her lips and stilled them. "The sight of you like that, so disheveled, stirred me," he said very quietly. "It isn't a thing that a gentleman should admit, and I was taking pains to conceal what I felt. I spoke in frustration. I didn't mean to hurt you."

She was horribly embarrassed now. "As if your opinion of my . . . of my body matters to me!"

"You have little enough self-esteem," he continued, as if she hadn't spoken at all. "It was unkind of me to do further damage to it." He brought her hand to his mouth and kissed it tenderly. "Forgive me."

She tried to pull her hand away. "Please . . . don't do that," she said breathlessly.

He looked into her eyes and held them with a suddenly glittery, piercing stare. "Does it disturb you to feel my mouth on your skin, Bernadette?" he chided very softly.

She was terribly uncomfortable and it was showing. The breathlessness now was as much excitement as asthma, and his expression told her that he knew it.

His thumb smoothed over the back of her hand in a slow, sensuous tracing that made the breathlessness worse. "You're far too innocent," he said huskily. "Like a Spanish maiden cloistered with her duenna. You understand your own feelings even less than you understand mine."

"I don't understand anything," she choked out.

"I realize that." His fingers moved to her mouth and slowly, gently, traced its soft outline in a silence that throbbed with excitement and dark promise.

It was the first intimate contact she'd ever had with a man and it unnerved her. "Eduardo," she whispered uncertainly.

His thumb pressed hard against her lips, parting them. Something flashed in his eyes as he felt her mouth tremble under the sudden rough caress of his thumb bruising the inside of her lips back against her teeth.

She gasped and he made a sound deep in his throat, somewhere between a groan and a growl.

The lace at her throat was shaking wildly. She saw his eyes go there and then, inexplicably, to her bodice. His breath drew in sharply. She looked down, curious even through her excitement, to see what had brought that sound from his lips.

She saw nothing except the sharp points of her nipples against the fabric, but why should that disturb him?

His eyes moved back up to hers. His fingers traced her chin and lifted it. His eyes fell to her soft mouth. He moved, just enough to bring him so close that she could taste the coffee scent and cigar smoke on his mouth as it hovered near hers.

She had a hold on his dark jacket. She didn't realize how tight a hold it was until she became aware of the cool cloth in her fingers.

"Bernadette," he whispered in a tone she'd never heard him use before. She was frozen in time, in space. She wanted his mouth to come down and cover hers. She wanted to taste it, as she'd wanted to so often in the past two years, even as she feared the change that it would bring to their turbulent relationship. But at the moment, the blood was surging through her veins and she was hungry for something she'd never known. The lack of restraint made her reckless.

Involuntarily, she leaned closer to him, her lips approaching his as she forgot all her upbringing in the heat of sudden desire.

He was tempted as he hadn't been in many years. He was painfully tempted. But suddenly, he murmured something violent in Spanish, something she was certain he'd never have given voice if he'd suspected how fluent she was in Spanish. She'd never told him that she had learned his language, for fear of him knowing the reason—that she wanted to speak it because it was his native tongue.

He drew back, his expression curiously taut and odd. He stared at her with narrowed eyes and she flushed at her own forward, outrageous behavior and dropped her gaze to his jacket in a flurry of embarrassment.

Tension flowed between them as the sudden sound of hard shoes on tile broke the pregnant silence like pistol shots. Eduardo moved away from her to the window and grasped the thick curtain in his lean hand as Maria came through the open doorway carrying a silver tray.

She was looking at it, not at the occupants of the room, so Bernadette had a few precious seconds to compose herself. Her hands still shook badly, but she managed to clasp them in her lap while Maria put the cups and saucers along with a pitcher of cream and a sugar dish on the table against the wall. She poured thick coffee into the cups and then laid napkins and spoons beside them. By the time she brought the coffee to Bernadette, the younger woman was pale but smiling. "Thank you, Maria," she said hoarsely, and tried to sip the hot coffee, almost burning her mouth in the process.

"This disease of the lungs is something you must be careful about, niña," Maria said firmly. "You must take better care of yourself. Is this not so, Señor Conde?"

He turned from the window and faced them with his usual composure. "Yes, it is," he agreed, although his voice sounded huskier than usual. "Will you stay with her, Maria?" he added curtly. "I'll go find her father myself. There's something I need to discuss with him."

"Do you not want your coffee?" she asked, surprised.

"Not at the moment, grácias." He barely glanced at Bernadette. With a courteous nod, he left the room.

"What odd behavior," Maria murmured.

Bernadette didn't say a word. She'd shamed herself so badly that she wondered if she'd ever be able to look Eduardo in the eye again. Why couldn't she have controlled her wild heartbeat, her scant but rapid breathing, when he was so close? How could she have leaned so close to him, as if she were begging him to kiss her?

She groaned aloud, and Maria hovered worriedly. "I'm all right," she assured the servant. "It's just that . . . that the coffee is hot," she said finally.

"This is so, but it will help your lungs," Maria coaxed with a smile.

Yes, it would help the lungs. Strong black coffee often stopped an attack of asthma stone cold.

But it wasn't going to do much for the renegade heart that was beating like a drum in her chest or the shame she'd brought on herself in a moment of ungoverned passion. Amazing that she could feel such emotions with Eduardo. He didn't even want her. But if he didn't, then why had he come so close, spoken so seductively? It was the first time since she'd known him that he'd ever behaved in that way with her. They fought constantly. But there were times when he had been tender with her, concerned for her, as even her own father wasn't. But this, today, was different. He'd treated her for the first time as a woman he desired. It gave her an extraordinary feeling of power, of maturity.

She let herself dream, for a space of seconds, that he felt the same helpless attraction for her that she felt for him. Only a dream, but so sweet!

Chapter Two

EDUARDO STALKED TOWARD THE BARN WHERE MARIA had said Colston Barron was working. He felt sick to his stomach for the way he'd worked on Bernadette's senses, taking advantage of her naivete and unworldliness. She was easy prey for an experienced man. He'd turned her inside out with no trouble at all, just to see if he could. The result made his head spin. She wanted him. He was dumbfounded. Having experienced little more than open hostility from her, especially for the past two years, the knowledge of her vulnerability with him was overwhelming.

His mind was forming plans as he walked. Bernadette's father wanted a titled son-in-law, a place in polite society that his wealth couldn't buy for him. Bernadette was ripe for a lover. Eduardo, on the other hand, needed money badly to save his ranch. The alternative was to go on his knees to his grandmother and beg for help, something the proud old woman might not give him—without strings attached. Her favorite was his cousin Luis, a shrewd young blade with big eyes and grandiose plans who would love to see Eduardo humbled.

Eduardo's mouth set into a thin line. He needed a rich wife. Bernadette needed a titled husband. Moreover, her father might be receptive to him. If he played his cards right, he could save his pride *and* his ranch. As for Bernadette, what little affection she might require he could surely force himself to give her. She was too young to know the difference between seduction and passionate love. He could make her happy. Her poor health would be a drawback, but no match was perfect. She might in time bear him a child, if the risk was not too great. He would ask only one of her, and pray that it would be a son to inherit the ranch.

He caught sight of the little Irishman talking to one of the stable hands. Colston Barron's red hair was mussed, and his red face with its big nose was framed by ears that didn't know to lie flat against his head. He was far from handsome, and he had no real breeding. His language was punctuated with expletives, and he had little patience. But he was a fair man and he was honest, traits Eduardo had always admired in his nearest neighbor.

The Irishman turned on his bow legs when he heard Eduardo approach, going forward to greet him with an outstretched hand and a grin.

"Well, Eduardo, sure and this is a hell of a time

of day to come visiting a poor working man! How are you, lad?"

"Very well, thank you," the younger man replied. His eyes narrowed thoughtfully. "Bernadette tells me you're planning a ball."

"Yes." He glared at the house. "One last desperate attempt to get her married and off me hands. She's twenty, you know, Eduardo, an invalid half the time, and a nuisance the rest. I have two men picked out for her. One is a German duke and the other's an Italian count. No money, of course," he added under his breath, "but old families and old names. She could do a hell of a lot worse, let me tell you! And there's not a reason in the world why I shouldn't benefit a bit from her marriage by acquiring a noble son-in-law. After all, I've spent a fortune keeping her alive over the years!"

The man's insensitivity disturbed Eduardo. "She has no wish to marry a title, or so she told me," he returned, and watched the other man fluster.

"She will damned well marry who I say," he burst out, going redder than ever. "The little ingrate! She needn't expect me to support her for the rest of her miserable life!"

Just for a second, Eduardo had a glimpse of what life must be like here for Bernadette, at her father's mercy because of her illness and with no place else to go. He might not love her, but if he married her, at least she would have freedom and some measure of independence.

"Anyway," Colston was calming a little now, "she'll marry if I say so. She has no choice. If I throw her out, where will she go, I ask you, in her condition? Her brother has a family of his own. He can't keep her. And it isn't as if she could go out to work."

Eduardo clasped his hands behind him as they walked. "These men of whom you speak—they wish to marry Bernadette?"

"Well, no," came the reluctant reply. "I've promised to finance renovations for their fine estate houses and pay off their debts. Still, they're not keen on an American wife, and a semi-invalid at that."

Eduardo stopped walking and turned to the smaller man. "She's not an invalid."

"Not most of the time," he replied, wary of the younger man's black temper, which he'd seen a time or two. "But she has weeks when she can't lift her head, usually in the spring and fall. She gets pneumonia every winter." He shifted. "Damned nuisance, she is. I have to pay a nurse to watch her night and day throughout the bouts."

Coming from a family that was tender with its invalids, Eduardo found Colston's attitude unbelievably callous, but he held his tongue.

"I have a proposition to put to you."

Colston held out a hand invitingly. "Please. Go right ahead, then."

"I have a title and quite an old family name. My grandmother is a direct descendant of the family of Isabella, Queen of Spain, and we have connections to most of the royal houses of Europe as well."

"Why, my dear lad, of course. There isn't a soul hereabouts that's unaware of your lineage—even though you never speak of it."

"There was no reason to, until now." He didn't add that he considered it bad manners to boast of such connections. Everyone in Valladolid County knew that he was only half Spanish, that his wife had died mysteriously, and that he was a count. Despite his title, he wouldn't be most men's choice for a son-in-law. But Colston Barron wanted royal connections, and even if his were a bit unusual, he still had them. He stared off into the distance, aware of his neighbor's unblinking stare. "If I married Bernadette, you would have the titled son-in-law and social acceptance you seek. On the other hand, I would have the desperately needed funds to save my ranch from bankruptcy."

Colston was struck dumb. He just stared, breathless, mindless, at the tall man beside him. After a minute he let out the breath he was holding. "You'd marry her? Her!"

Muscles clenched all over Eduardo's body at the

way the man referred to his daughter, but he nodded.

"I'll be damned!"

Eduardo didn't reply. He looked down at Bernadette's unloving father and waited.

Colston let out another rush of breath and put a hand to his forehead. "Well, this comes as a shock. I mean, you and the girl don't even like each other. You fight all the time."

"It would be a merger," he pointed out, "not a love match. Bernadette will be cared for."

"But, man, you'll want an heir. She can't give you a child!"

Eduardo's brows drew together. "Why?"

"Her mother and her older sister both died in childbirth," Colston said. "The girl is terrified of having a child. It's the reason she fights me so hard about arranging a marriage for her. You didn't know?"

Eduardo shook his head. He looked worried, and he was. "I assumed that she didn't want to be forced to marry a man only because he had a title."

"It's a little more complicated than that, I'm afraid." Colston sighed heavily. "She's not as frail as her mother and sister, even with her weak lungs. But she has an unnatural fear of childbirth, and with good cause. You might never be able to—" The older man stopped and coughed uncomfortably. "Well, I'm sure you understand."

There was a long silence. It was a disappointment, but it still didn't alter the facts. If Eduardo didn't do something, and soon, he was going to lose Rancho Escondido for good. He could live without a son for the time being. Later on, after he had his precious heritage safe from the bankers and the courts, he could worry about Bernadette's aversion to pregnancy.

"I would still like to marry her," Eduardo said.

Colston was shocked and delighted. "My dear boy," he said, grasping Eduardo's hand to shake it fervently. "My dear boy, I can't tell you how happy you've made me!"

"It won't make her happy," Eduardo pointed out solemnly. "And I think it would be best not to mention to her that we've spoken."

"I see. You want to win her."

Eduardo shrugged. "I will court her," he corrected. "Formally and very correctly. There is no need to make her feel like a bargain bride in the process."

"It won't be easy," Colston said. "She's already run off one prospective suitor," he recalled darkly. "Damned little nuisance that she is, she takes pleasure in defying me! She's a prickly thing at best."

Eduardo knew that, but he was remembering what had happened in the living room. Bernadette was vulnerable to him physically. He could play on that attraction, use it to win her. It wasn't going to be particularly hard, either. He felt like something of a blackguard for arranging things this way, but he was running out of choices. He could never work for wages or go begging to his grandmother for money. If he lost the ranch, those would be his only choices. He would rather slit his own throat.

"What do you want me to do?" Colston asked suddenly.

"Invite me to the ball, of course," came the dry reply. "I'll handle the rest."

"Done!"

Bernadette, totally unaware of the plotting that was going on around her, got over her asthma attack and helped Maria in the kitchen.

"Ah, el conde is such a man," Maria said, still dreamy as she made bread in the old wooden bread tray. "Such a man. And he carried you into the house in his arms."

Bernadette colored, embarrassed. "I was faint," she said curtly. "The pollen in my flowers had reduced me to coughing spasms that I couldn't control." She shifted as she stacked plates. "Besides, you know that there's nothing between me and Eduardo. He doesn't like me."

"Liking is not always a necessity, señorita. Sometimes it is an obstacle." She glanced at the other woman mischieviously. "He is very handsome, is he not?"

"Compared to what?"

"Señorita!" Maria was shocked. "Surely you

would find him more suited to your taste than some of these pendejos that your father invites here in the hope of marrying you off."

Bernadette toyed with a fork. Her eyes were sad with recollections of them. "Dukes and counts and earls," she murmured. "And not all of them lumped together would make one good man." She shook her head. "I don't want to be sold to some man for a title, just so my father can rub elbows with people like the Rockefellers and the Astors." She glanced at Maria. "He doesn't understand. You have to be born into those circles. You can't belong to them just because you've got a little money. My father isn't a cultured man. He's what they call a jump-up. He'll never move in the circles of high society, regardless of how well I marry. Why can't he be happy among people who like him?"

"Always a man seeks at least one thing that he cannot have," Maria said philosophically. "I suppose we must have dreams."

"Yes. Even women." She smiled thoughtfully. "You know, I'd like to be able to go to the theater unescorted, or sit in a restaurant alone, or go mountain climbing. I'd like to wear trousers and cut off my hair and work at a job." She saw the other woman's shocked face and laughed. "You think I'm crazy, don't you?"

"These things," Maria said uncomfortably, "are for men."

"They should be for everyone. Why should men have all the rights? Why should they be able to make slaves of women? Why should they have the right to keep us from voting, from helping to make the laws that govern us? I keep all the books for my father, I tell him when to buy and when to sell, I even handle the budget. He admits that I do an excellent job as bookkeeper, but does he pay me for my work? No. Family, he says, doesn't pay family for helping out!" She pointed a finger at Maria. "You mark my words, one day there'll be an uprising against all this injustice." She was getting too emotionally aroused. Her chest began to feel clogged and she started coughing.

Maria poured coffee quickly into a dainty china cup and handed it to Bernadette. "Here. Drink it. Rapidamente . . . rapidamente."

Bernadette did, barely able to get several swallows down her convulsing throat. She sat and bent forward, hating the spells that kept her from being a normal woman.

"There. It is better?" Maria asked a few moments later.

"Yes." Bernadette took a slow, careful breath and sat up. She looked at Maria ruefully. "I guess I'd better be less emotional about my ideas."

"It might help."

She put a hand to her chest. "I wonder how it is that Eduardo knows what to do when I have an attack?" she asked, because his careful handling of her had been puzzling.

"Because he asked me and I told him," Maria said simply. "It disturbed him that he came upon you once in this condition and had to get your father to tend you. You remember," she continued irritably, "your father was entertaining a friend and he was very angry that he had to be interrupted. He and el conde had words about this, although you were never told." She shrugged. "Afterward, el conde came to me and asked what to do for you. He was furious at your father for his insensitivity."

Bernadette's heart jumped. "How odd. I mean, he doesn't even like me."

"That is not so," Maria said with a gentle smile. "He is tender with you. It is something one notices, because he has little patience with most people. My Juan says that the other vaqueros are very careful not to annoy el conde, because his temper is something of a legend. He never seems to lose it with you."

"That doesn't stop him from mocking me, from being sarcastic. We argue all the time."

"Perhaps he does it because you treat him in the same way. And he may not want you to know that he likes you."

"Ha!"

Maria made a face at her. "All the same, he is kind to you."

"When it suits him." Bernadette didn't want to think about how she'd behaved with Eduardo earlier. It embarrassed her to recall how close she'd come to begging him to kiss her. She had to make sure that they weren't alone again. It wouldn't do to have him pity her. Better to keep him from ever finding out how violent were her feelings for him.

Her father did not return to the house until long after Eduardo had left. He paused to check on the repainting of the ballroom before he joined his daughter in the living room.

Giving her a hard look, he went to pour himself a brandy. "Eduardo said you were feeling poor," he said stiffly. He never seemed to unbend with her, as he used to with her brother. There was always distance between them.

"Yes, I was," she replied calmly. "But as you see, I'm better now. It was only the pollen from the flowers. It bothers my lungs."

"Along with dust, perfume, cold air, and ten thousand other things," he said coldly. He stared at her over the brandy snifter, his small eyes narrowed and calculating. "I expect you to dress appropriately for the ball. You can take the carriage and go to town, I'll have Rudolfo drive you. Buy something expensive, something that makes you look the daughter of a wealthy man." He waved a hand at the plain, blue calico dress she was wearing. "Something that doesn't look homemade," he added.

She stiffened, wishing with all her heart that she could tell him what she really thought of his treatment of her. But she had no choice at the moment. If her situation ever changed, she promised herself, this self-important little jackass was going to get an earful!

"It was you who told me to make my own clothes so that I wouldn't be a financial burden on you, Father," she said.

He colored. "The whole purpose of this ball is to find you a husband!"

"And you a titled son-in-law!" she said, rising to her feet with bristling fury. "So that you can mingle with the 'right sort of people.' "

"Don't you speak to me like that!" he said furiously.

"Then don't you treat me like a disease you might catch!" she returned, green eyes sparkling with temper. "I can't help it that I've got bad lungs, and I never asked to be born! I don't need second sight to know that you blame me for my mother's death!"

He took a sharp breath and seemed to grow two inches. "Sure and that's just what you did," he said through his teeth. "You killed her."

"Through no fault of my own," she replied. Her heartbeat was so rapid and forceful that it was making her whole body shake. She could barely breathe. She hated arguing. It brought on the dreaded attacks. But she wasn't going to back down. "You won't get her back by treating me like your worst enemy, either."

He took a huge swallow of brandy and let out a rough sigh. "I loved her more than my own life," he said almost to himself. "She was the most beautiful woman I ever saw. I never could understand what she saw in me, but she was the very heart of me. Then you came," he added, turning to her with eyes as cold as they had been tender when he spoke of his late wife. "And my Eloise was gone forever."

"It wasn't my fault," she said.

He glared at her. "It wasn't anyone else's," he retorted. He finished his brandy and put down the snifter. "Well, I may have lost my treasure, but I'll get some satisfaction from seeing you properly wed." He gave her a long, calculating look. "I've invited two European noblemen to the ball."

"Both impoverished, no doubt," she said mockingly.

The glare was more fierce. "They both come from fine European families and they need wives. And so help me, if you dare to embarrass me as you did the last time—blacking your teeth and wearing pants, for the love of Christ!—I will—"

"It was your own fault," she interrupted with more courage than she actually felt. It didn't do to show weakness to this man. "You can tell your new candidates that they needn't look for a wife here," she said stubbornly.

"They can and they will. You'll marry who I say," he told her in an uncompromising tone. "You can rant and rave all you like, but you'll do it! Otherwise," he added harshly, "I'll put you out, so help me, I will!"

She couldn't believe she was hearing this. Her face went deathly white as she stared at him with eyes like saucers. "Would you, then?" she returned. "And who'd keep your books and balance your accounts, pay your bills, and keep you to a budget so the ranch is financially sound?"

His fists clenched by his side. "I fought off Indians and Northerners and people who hated me because I was Irish, when I worked on the railroads! And yet even all that was less trouble than you give me every day of me life! You took Eloise from me! Does bookkeeping make up for that?"

She sat down, and stared at him, praying that her lungs wouldn't go into spasm yet again. You could never show weakness in front of the enemy!

Colston let out the breath that was choking him. Only then did he seem to realize what he'd said to her. He moved to the window and looked out, his back ramrod stiff. "That was a bit harsh," he bit off. "I wouldn't really throw you out. You're me only daughter, in spite of everything. But don't go against me, girl," he cautioned. "I mean to have respectability, and there's nothing I won't do to get it. You'll marry!"

"A man I don't even know." She was fighting tears of rage and impotence. "A stranger who'll take me to some cold foreign country to die."

He whirled. "Sure and you won't die, you little fool!" he exclaimed. "You'll have maids and other servants to look after you. Someone to cook and clean for you. You'll be treated like a queen!"

"I'll be an interloper," she returned. "Unwanted and hated because I've been married for *your* money!"

He threw up his hands. "I offer you the world, and you want to put labels on everything!"

She was dying inside. He was going to sell her, and she'd never see Eduardo again. Never, never . . .

"There is an alternative," he said after a minute.

She looked up.

He studied his boots, caked with mud. "You might consider marrying Eduardo."

Her heart went right up into her throat. She put a hand to it, to keep it from jumping out onto the floor. "Wh . . . what?"

"Eduardo!" He stared at her, planted with feet wide and both hands behind his back. "He's a widower, and what polite society would call a half-breed, but he does have a title. His family is connected to European royalty."

She laughed, almost choking in the process.

"Eduardo wouldn't want me," she said bitterly. "He hates me."

"He might be willing to marry you," he continued, careful not to mention the conversation he'd had with the man. "Especially if you tried to improve yourself a little, if you dressed up and smiled at him once in a while. He'll have competition at the ball. Two other men, both titled. It might make him sit up." He looked away, so that she couldn't see the unholy glee in his eyes. He'd frightened her enough that Eduardo now looked like salvation itself. He congratulated himself silently on his shrewdness. So much for her stubborn refusal to consider a match of his choosing. She could be won over, with the right words and strategies.

"He's said that he doesn't want to remarry," she continued.

"He's also said that he doesn't want to lose his inheritance," he reminded her. "If his past wasn't so unpleasant, his old grandmother could help him make another match in Spain, as she did with his late wife. But his wife died under mysterious circumstances and his mother has become embroiled in some new scandal back east. She isn't Spanish at all—his mother is a Texas heiress who comes from German and good Irish stock."

"I know that. She lives in New York with her second husband. Eduardo hates her."

He didn't know how she knew that, but he didn't

push his luck. He folded his arms over his chest. "It's because of what his mother's done that his grandmother is determined to leave her wealth to his second cousin. Not only is he completely Spanish, but he has no scandal about him."

"Eduardo told you that?"

He nodded. "Some time ago, of course," he added evasively. "They say the old lady's coming here to stay with him for the summer."

"He'll be glad, I imagine. He loves his grandmother."

"Pity it isn't mutual." His small eyes riveted themselves to her face. "Well, what do you think of marrying Eduardo?"

She swallowed. "I would . . . be willing, I suppose," she said with just the right touch of reluctance, "if it would save me from having to live in some foreign place."

He felt like dancing a jig, but he didn't dare let his stubborn daughter know how much her acceptance pleased him. Sometimes he even liked her for her spirit—so long as he didn't remember what she'd cost him with her birth. Honest to God, she was almost a mirror image of him in temper. "Then suppose you go into town as I suggested and find a nice gown to wear to the ball?"

She drew in a long breath. "I suppose I could do that."

"Go to Meriwether's, where I have an account. Buy whatever you need."

She stood up. "Eduardo's title is only good in Europe," she began.

He held up a hand. "It's good anywhere," he said stiffly. "Even in Texas. He's only half Spanish, but most people will overlook that because of his European relations." He gave her a long, unpleasant look. "Considering your lack of beauty and the state of your health, I really think it would be overly optimistic to think that a European would want you. We'll be lucky indeed if Eduardo is willing to take you on."

"I'm not so much a burden as you like to think, Father. I do earn my keep. I'm quite good with figures and budgets. Eduardo might even find me an asset, given his present circumstances."

He shrugged. "You're useful enough, when you're well. But you're quite often sick, Bernadette." He turned away heavily. "It's the memories you bring back," he said in a rare moment's honesty. "I see her face as she died, hear her scream, feel my heart break and break inside my body." He put a hand absently to his chest. "I loved her so!"

Bernadette actually felt the words. But before she could speak, he turned and went out the door, his footsteps loud and angry, as they always were when he had to confront something unpleasant or irritating.

She stared after him in misery. If he'd turned to her instead of away from her, how different her life might have been. He blamed her for his wife's death, would always blame her. She could never hope for a closer relationship with him, because he didn't want one. All he wanted from his daughter was an advantageous marriage and her complete absence from his life. He didn't say that, but he meant it.

She felt very old as she went to get her hat and gloves. She had few choices left now, but she was going to get out of her father's life. She couldn't bring herself to marry a European. She would love to marry Eduardo. But that, despite her father's curious interest in the subject, was unlikely. Eduardo's aversion to a second marriage was well known to everyone. Her father would never persuade him to go through with such a venture, and certainly she wasn't going to be able to seduce their neighbor into marriage with her pitiful assets.

Still, letting her father think it could happen might keep him from pressuring her about his other candidates.

For an instant, she let herself dream about how it would be to marry Eduardo and openly show her love for him, to be loved by him in return. She felt a powerful physical attraction to him that was profoundly augmented by the deep love she felt for him. He had no such interest in her, although he seemed to find her physically attractive.

She wondered if she could really heighten that interest. She knew very little of men, but she was a great reader of forbidden books, and she did know how to dress and behave in public. Some of the girls at her exclusive finishing school in New York had talked quite candidly about their relationships with men. But Bernadette, while spirited, was a novice. Eduardo could do anything with her, and she dared not lure him into a position where she might fall from grace.

But the mere thought that he might be willing to marry her was so intriguing a proposition that her heart was skipping beats. It was the first time she'd been able to see marriage as a real possibility in her life. Despite her father's manipulations, she might permit herself to be convinced. If Eduardo was interested in marrying her at all, she might be the very person who could help him reorganize his ranch and make it show a profit. Her father didn't like being reminded that she'd saved him from a drastic financial loss once, several years before when she first took over the enormous task of overseeing the accounts after the resignation of their bookkeeper. Her father had liked the idea of not paying an outsider, or allowing a stranger to see his assets. But whether Eduardo would want to marry her, even for her father's money, remained to be seen. It also gave her hope that, if she had courage, her wildest dreams might come true.

Chapter Three

BERNADETTE FOUND HERSELF IN THE EXCLUSIVE Meriwether's Dry Goods Store with no clear idea of what she was going to buy.

The brother of the owner, Mr. Clem Meriwether, who'd been the head clerk for as long as Bernadette could remember, met her at the door with a wide smile.

"Lovely to see you again, Miss Barron," he said formally. "What can I help you with today?"

"My father sent me for a ball gown, Mr. Meriwether," she said. "I don't quite know—"

"But I have just the thing!" He chuckled as he led her inside. "And what a coincidence that it should arrive today. It's from Paris, an original design which was intended for one of the Carson girls in Fort Worth, but she declined to accept it, and it was sent to us on consignment. I had no idea that anyone here would want it. We're so distant from real society . . ." He turned and his ears seemed to go red. "Begging your pardon, miss,

I never meant that your father wasn't social or anything!"

"Think nothing of it, Mr. Meriwether," she said with a gentle smile. "I didn't take offense." She didn't think it prudent to add that her father would have gone right through the roof and cancelled his account if he'd heard what the nice man had said.

"We heard about this ball he's giving next month. Is it true that the Culhanes are coming all the way from El Paso?"

"Well, the parents, anyway," she amended. "We understand that two of the three sons are vacationing together on a cruise, leaving one behind to watch the ranch property."

"Still, it's something of an honor for any of the Culhanes to travel so far for a party, yes?"

"Yes, it is," she had to concede. "They're staying at the ranch for a week, of course, along with the other guests."

"Any other Texans on the guest list?" he probed gently as he took an elegantly trimmed box from a shelf.

"I'm not really sure," she replied. "Father's kept very quiet about his guest list. I think he wants to surprise me," she added with just the right touch of mischief.

"That's understandable. Is it your birthday?"

She shook her head. "It's no real occasion," she

lied, not wanting to admit that her father was holding the ball primarily to auction off his daughter to the man with the most impressive title. "Just Father's idea of a summer diversion, although he is saying that it's a celebration of his new railroad acquisition."

"So much the better." He put the box down on the counter, opened it with a flourish, and drew out the most exquisite gown Bernadette had ever seen in her life. She stopped breathing at the sight of it.

He chuckled. "No need to ask if you like it. If you'll wait a moment, Miss Barron, I'll get my wife to come and help you try it on."

He stepped to the back of the store and called for Maribeth, a small, cheerful woman who came right along, drying her hands on a cloth.

"I've been putting up bread-and-butter pickles, Miss Barron. I'll save you two or three jars for when you come next time."

"Why, thank you!" Bernadette said, surprised by the offer.

"It's nothing at all. Now, let me help you with this dress. Isn't it lovely? And Clem never thought anyone around here would need such a grand gown! It's actually from Paris, France, you know!"

The little woman babbled on as she led Bernadette back to the makeshift fitting room and helped her into the gown. It took awhile, because there seemed to be a hundred tiny buttons to fasten. But once the gown was on, Bernadette knew that she'd have sold anything she owned to get enough money to buy it.

It was white, a delicious concoction of soft material that fell to her ankles in layers of lace and georgette, festooned by pink silk flowers and tiny blue bows. The bodice was draped with the same soft georgette and tiny puffed sleeves echoed the motif. Her shoulders were left bare and the tops of her pretty breasts were just visible. It was a seductive dress without being vulgar. Bernadette looked at herself in the mirror with pure awe.

"Is that me?" she asked, her heart pounding with excitement.

"Oh, my, yes," Mrs. Meriwether said with a sigh. "What a delightful fit, and how it suits you! You must leave your hair down and tie it in back with a pink silk ribbon, my dear. I'll show you how."

"I've never worn my hair down," she said doubtfully.

"It will be perfect with this gown. Here. Let me show you."

She took down Bernadette's elaborate coiffure and replaced it with a simpler one, offset by the pink satin ribbon she made from a length of the silky material. "There," she said when she finished. "Do you see what I mean? It's perfect with the dress."

"Indeed it is," Bernadette had to admit. She looked young and elegant and somehow vulnerable. She almost looked pretty. She smiled at herself and was surprised by the change it made in her rather ordinary features.

"And a fan to go with it," the little woman was mumbling. "Where did I put that silk one . . . aha!"

She produced a fan so pretty that Bernadette fell in love with it at once. It was made of pale pink silk with elegant patterns of flowers, outlined in ivory lace. It was the most beautiful fan she'd ever seen.

"And these gloves, and that little purse. You'll need shoes. Let's see what we have. . . ."

It was the most exciting hour of Bernadette's life. By the time she had her purchases wrapped up and was ready to leave, she felt as if she'd been let out of prison. The ball would be the crowning glory of her life, despite her father's matchmaking. She couldn't wait to see the look on Eduardo's face when he saw her!

Her father didn't trust Bernadette to make the arrangements for his ball, so he'd assigned them to Mrs. Maude Carlisle, a former social secretary to one of the Astors in New York, and the wife of a prominent retired army officer in San Antonio. Mrs. Carlisle was staying with friends in Valladolid for several weeks and she was overjoyed to help Mr. Barron plan his grand fete.

She knew exactly how to go about organizing things on a monumental scale, and she set to work at once. Two weeks later, she'd alienated half the staff on the Barron ranch. This didn't bother Colston one bit. But Bernadette was overwhelmed with complaints. Everyone including Maria cried on her shoulder while the painstaking arrangements were made. There was a bakery to cater the confections, a local cook to cater the finger foods for the hors d'oeuvre table, and flowers purchased from a greenhouse. No detail was overlooked or left undone. Bernadette did her best to stay out of the way of the ongoing madness.

She put on her riding skirt and had the stable boy saddle her pretty bay mare for her. She'd just mounted when her father came into the barn.

"And where are you going?" he demanded. "Mrs. Carlisle needs you to talk to Maria about the dinnerware."

"Why?" she asked with some surprise.

"Maria's suddenly forgotten how to speak English, that's why!"

Silently, Bernadette applauded her friend's initiative. That was one way to get around Mrs. Carlisle. "You know I don't speak Spanish," she lied without meeting his eyes. Actually, she'd kept her knowledge of that tongue a secret from her father as well as Eduardo, because it gave her a definite advantage when dealing with her father. She could talk to the staff in their own language whenever she liked. He couldn't. He spoke only Gaelic and English.

"You could convince Maria at least to talk to the poor woman!"

"I'm going riding, Father," she said. "I must get some fresh air in my lungs."

He glared at her with suspicion. "You're running away. It won't do any good. Klaus Branner and Carlo Maretti are due here tomorrow on the train from Houston."

Her heart jumped and she felt suddenly sick. "I've told you how I feel about this," she said stiffly.

"And I've told you how I feel," he said narrowly. "Eduardo hasn't been near the place in two weeks," he added, and refused to let her know how that worried him. He didn't think much of her abilities to attract Europeans, but Eduardo had this way of looking at her just recently. He liked Eduardo, too, and respected him. It would have been the ideal match. He wondered why Eduardo had apparently changed his mind after their discussion. "It seems that he's no longer in the running, my girl, so it's my two candidates, or else."

What he said was true. Eduardo hadn't come to call, which was very unusual for him, and Bernadette had worried herself sick about the reasons. It was impossible to invite herself to his ranch, so she waited in vain for him and watched her dreams disintegrate. She knew that without the hope of Eduardo as a suitor, her father would turn quickly to his other two candidates. As he had.

Bernadette stared down at him with a drawn face. "Maybe they won't want me," she said daringly.

"They'll want you," he replied tersely. "Because they want my money!"

She made one last attempt to reason with him. "Don't you care if I'm happy or not, Father?" she asked miserably. "Don't you care at all?"

His face closed up, went tight and hard. "I'm not happy," he pointed out. "I've been alone and miserable for twenty years because of you!"

Her features contorted. "You aren't blameless!"

He looked as if he might explode. "How dare you speak to me in such a way!" he blustered. "How dare you!"

Her lower lip trembled. She gripped her riding crop more firmly, until her knuckles went white. "I hope I never live long enough to treat a child of mine the way you've treated me," she said huskily. "And I hope you live long enough to be sorry for it."

He pulled himself up to his full height and glared at her. "That day will never come."

She turned her horse and rode away, leaving him standing alone.

She couldn't remember ever feeling quite so low and desperate. Eduardo was out of her reach, and her father's candidates were to arrive the following day. She wondered if she could run away without being caught. It was a poor way to cope, but she knew that other young women in similar predicaments had done such things. If all else failed, it was one workable solution, even if her precarious state of health made it impractical.

She was deep in thought, without any real idea of where she was going. This area of south Texas was mostly scrub brush and cacti, sand and dust and heat, even in the spring. But she loved the sense of freedom it gave her with all that long empty horizon in front of her. It was like looking at the stars at night; it made her little problems seem very insignificant. Right now, she needed that most of all. The imminent arrival of two titled Europeans made her sick to her stomach. Perhaps they wouldn't like her. But if they needed money badly enough, they'd probably be willing to marry a scarecrow, a cow, anyone. Even her.

She guided the little mare toward the stream that crossed her father's land. There were a few willow trees there, along with mesquite and some poplars. The leaves were the soft, pale green of new growth, and there was a breeze. It wasn't as smoldering hot as it usually was, either. She dismounted under a big mesquite tree and tossed her flat-brimmed hat to one side as she bent to wet her handkerchief in the stream.

Birds called overhead and she wondered at their sudden burst of noise just as she heard hoofbeats approaching.

She turned, moving closer to her mount. It was a lonely place, and there were often bandits about. But as the rider approached, she recognized him at once and sighed with relief. As usual, a thrill of sheer joy went stabbing through her at the sight of him. He sat a horse like a soldier, very straight and proud, and she loved just looking at him.

"What are you doing out here alone?" Eduardo called curtly as he drew close.

His words breaking the spell she seemed to be under, she smiled ruefully. "I'm escaping Mrs. Carlisle."

His eyebrows arched under the wide brim of his hat and he smiled. "Mrs. Carlisle?"

"She's organizing the grand ball," she informed him. "I'm trying to stay out of her way. So is everybody else. The whole staff may resign any minute now."

"Shouldn't your out-of-town guests be arriving soon?"

"My father's handpicked matrimonial candidates arrive tomorrow," she said with undisguised revulsion. "One's German, the other's Italian."

"He invited them, then," he murmured under his breath. This was a surprise. Colston Barron hadn't seemed interested in other candidates for

Bernadette's dowry the last time he'd spoken with the man. Of course, he'd avoided the place like the plague since then. Guilt had kept him away; it disturbed him to think of using Bernadette for his own ends. He was ashamed of himself, of his less than noble motives, wooing a woman he didn't love for the sake of financial gain. It was dishonest at best, and he was too honorable not to be suffering from a bad conscience.

"Of course he invited them," Bernadette replied. She glanced at him sadly, with faint accusation. "You're not one of his prospective hopefuls, by the way, in case you were wondering. That should be of some comfort to you."

He pulled a cigar case from his shirt pocket and extracted one of the Cuban cigars he favored. He produced a small box of matches and lit it before he spoke. "I see."

She wondered why he should suddenly look so thoughtful, so tense. He turned away and she studied his profile. Could he be upset because he wasn't a candidate for her hand? She didn't dare hope so. But what if he was?

He felt her avid gaze and turned to meet it. She colored prettily. "How are you going to feel about living abroad?" he asked.

"It's that or find some way to support myself," she said wearily. "My father says either I get married or I get out."

"Surely not!" he exclaimed angrily.

"Well, he threatened to do it," she replied. She rubbed the mare's soft muzzle absently. "He's determined to have his way in this."

"And will you do what you're told, Bernadette?" he asked quietly.

She looked up at him, red-cheeked. "No, I will not! Not if I have to take a job as a shop girl somewhere or work in a factory!"

"Your lungs would never survive a job in a cotton mill," he said softly.

"The alternative is to be someone's servant," she replied miserably. "I couldn't hold up to do that, either. Not for long." She leaned her cheek against the horse's long nose with a sigh. "Why can't time stand still, or go backward?" she asked in a haunted tone. "Why couldn't I be whole instead of sickly?"

"I can't believe that any father would cast off his daughter just because she refused to marry a candidate of his own choosing," he said irritably.

"Isn't it done in Spanish families all the time?"

He dismounted, cigar in hand, and moved to stand beside her. He was so much taller that she had to toss her head back to see his lean, dark face when he was this close.

"Yes, it is," he replied. "In fact, my marriage was the result of such an arrangement. But American families usually don't make those kinds of choices."

"That's what you think," she replied. "It's done all the time in the wealthier families. I knew a girl at finishing school who was forced to marry some rich French vintner, and she hated him on sight. She ran away, but they brought her back and made her go through with the ceremony."

"Made her?"

She hesitated to tell him why. It was vaguely scandalous and one didn't speak of such things in public, much less to men.

"Tell me," he prompted.

"Well, he kept her out all night," she said reluctantly. "She swore that nothing happened, but her family said she was ruined and had to marry him. No other decent man would have her after that, you see."

His dark gaze slid down her slender form in the riding habit and he began to smile in a way he never had before. "How innovative," he murmured.

"I went to the ceremony," Bernadette continued. "I felt so sorry for her. She was in tears at her own wedding, but her father was strutting. Her new husband was a member of the old French nobility, the part that didn't die in the Revolution and was later restored to its former glory."

"Did she learn to accept this match?" he probed.

Her eyes clouded. "She hurled herself overboard on the ship taking them to France," she said, and shivered. "Her body washed up on shore several days later. They said her father went mad afterward. She was his only child, and his wife was long dead. I felt sorry for him, but nobody else did."

Eduardo smoked his cigar and stared at the muddy water of the stream. There had been a good rain the day before, and the ground was soaked. He felt oddly betrayed by what he'd heard. He wondered why Bernadette's father had such a quick change of heart. Perhaps he realized that Eduardo wouldn't be easily led in business, or perhaps he felt that a man who was half-Spanish wasn't the sort of connection he wanted to have. It stung Eduardo to think that Colston might feel he wasn't good enough to marry his daughter.

"I'm sorry if I've embarrassed you," she said after a long silence had fallen between them.

He gave her a level look. "You haven't," he said. "Why does your father care so little about your happiness, Bernadette?"

She glanced away, her gaze resting on the river. "I thought you must have heard long ago. My mother died having me," she said. "He's blamed me ever since for killing her."

He made a rough sound in his throat. "What nonsense! God decides matters of life and death."

She turned her gaze back on him. "My father doesn't believe in Him, either," she said with resignation. "He lost his faith along with my mother. All he believes in now is making money and getting a title in the family."

"What a desolate, bitter life."

She nodded.

He thought she looked very neat in her riding habit. Her hair was carefully pinned so that the wind barely had disarranged it. He'd always liked the way she sat a horse, too. His late wife could ride side saddle, but she could barely stay on. Bernadette rode like a cowboy.

"What are you doing out here?" she asked suddenly.

A corner of his mouth turned up. "Looking for strays. I can't afford the loss of a single calf in my present financial situation."

She frowned slightly. "Your mother married a millionaire, didn't she?"

His eyes flickered, and his face went taut. "I don't discuss my mother."

She held up a hand. "I know. I'm sorry. It's just that I thought since she got the ranch into its present difficulties with her spending, she might be willing to make amends."

He didn't soften. "She wouldn't lift a finger to save it, or me," he said coldly. "She held my father in contempt because he wouldn't let her give lavish parties and have a houseful of guests staying for the summer. She drove him to such despair that he died . . . of a broken heart, I think, but I was young, only eight," he mused, a terrible look in his eyes as he remembered the scene all too vividly. "My mother was with her latest lover at the time, so I was sent to Spain, to live with my grandmother in Granada. When I was old enough, I came back here to reclaim my father's legacy." He shook his head. "I had no idea what a struggle it was going to be. Not that knowing would have stopped me," he added.

She was fascinated by this glimpse at something very personal in his life. "They say that your great-grandfather built the ranch on an old Spanish land grant."

"So he did," he replied.

"Did your mother love your father?"

He shrugged. "She loved jewelry and parties and scandal," he said through his teeth. "Embarrassing my father was her greatest pleasure in life. She adored notoriety." He stared at her. "Your father said that your elder sister, as well as your mother, died in childbirth."

Uncomfortable, she averted her eyes. Her hands clenched on the mare's bridle. "Yes."

He moved closer. "He also said that you're afraid of it."

Her eyes closed. She laughed without mirth. "Afraid? I'm terrified. It's why I don't want to marry. I don't want to die." It was true. Even her daydreams about Eduardo always ended with a chaste kiss, nothing more. Oddly, it didn't occur to her to wonder why her father should have told him such a personal thing about the family.

Eduardo was studying her. She was slight, yes, he thought, but she had wide hips and she was sturdy. Surely the asthma would be infinitely more dangerous than her build in the matter of childbirth.

"Not every woman has a hard time with childbirth," he said. "My late wife was much thinner than you, Bernadette, and she had an easy labor."

She didn't like talking about his wife. Her hand let go of the bridle. "I'll bet she didn't have a mother and a sister who both died that way."

"She was an only child. Her mother is still alive."

She turned, glancing at him. "Do you ever see her?"

He shook his head curtly.

"But, why?"

He didn't want to talk about this, but it was unavoidable. Bernadette drew information out of him that no one else could have. "She was . . . put away."

Her eyes widened. "Put away?"

"Yes." A terrible look came into his eyes. "She's quite mad."

Her intake of breath was audible. "Heavens!"

He looked down at her. "Go ahead. Ask me," he

challenged when he saw her hesitation. "Surely you don't mean to stop before you find out if my wife was deranged as well?"

Her gaze fell before the anger in his. "I'm sorry. I don't have the right to ask you such a thing."

"When has that ever held you back?"

She colored. "Sorry," she murmured again, and moved to remount the mare.

His lean hand caught her just as she lifted her foot toward the stirrup. He turned her and then let his hand fall. His eyes searched hers. "Consuela was quiet and introspective and very dignified," he said at last. "If there was madness in her, it only surfaced once. And about that, I never speak," he added tersely.

"Did you love her?" she asked with soft, curious eyes.

"I married her because my grandmother chose her for me, Bernadette," he replied. His chin went up. "It was to be a merging of fortunes, a family alliance. Sadly, I had little of my father's fortune left, and none of my mother's. Consuela's family had suffered devastating losses at their vineyards because of drought and a disastrous fire that killed the vines. Both families saw in me a way to mend the old fortunes. But there was too much against me."

She wanted to comfort him, but she couldn't think of a dignified way to do it. "How . . . how awful," she said. "I guess the ranch means a lot to you."

"It's all that I have left of my own."

"You'd do anything to save it, wouldn't you?" she asked in a subdued tone.

"Not anything," he said, and realized that it was true. He wasn't going to pretend to be in love with Bernadette to get her to marry him. "Although a good marriage would probably save me from bankruptcy," he added with faint insinuation.

She touched the saddle with a nervous hand. "Do you have a candidate in mind?"

"Oh, yes," he said. That, at least, was the truth. "Here, let me help you mount."

He assisted her into the saddle and rested his hand just beside her thigh while he looked up at her thoughtfully.

"Don't come here alone again," he cautioned. "There are bad men in the world, and you aren't strong."

She lifted the reins in her gloved hand. "Teddy Roosevelt had asthma as a child, you know," she said. "He went to Cuba with his own regiment and fought bravely, and now he's governor of New York State."

"You're thinking of following in his footsteps?"

She glanced down at him and chuckled softly. "No, I didn't mean that. I only meant that if he could overcome such an illness, perhaps I can, too."

"Nothing mends weak lungs," he said. "You must take care of yourself."

"I won't need to do that. My father has chosen two impoverished noblemen to do it for me."

He studied her thoughtfully. "Don't let him push you into anything you don't want," he said, suddenly vehement. "Life is far too short to be tied to a mate with whom you have nothing in common."

"Fine words coming from you," she shot back. "You let yourself be railroaded into marriage."

His eyes narrowed. "I didn't see it that way. I stand to inherit a fortune at my grandmother's death, all the family lands and vineyards in Andalusia and my grandmother's share of an inheritance. It was thought that an alliance with Consuela's family would simply increase the inheritance for our children and therefore ensure the future prosperity of the entire family. But these days my grandmother looks with more favor on my cousin Luis, who also married to please her and who has a son."

She stared at him blankly. "Would it hurt you to lose her money?"

He seemed hard at that moment, harder than she'd ever seen him.

"Not at all, if I could save my ranch. If I can't, I might end up as a vaquero working for wages." His eyes went dead. "I'd rather steal food than beg for it. An advantageous marriage would spare me that, at least."

She was mildly shocked. “I never thought of you as an opportunist.”

He laughed coldly. “I’m not, as a rule. But lately I’ve become a realist,” he corrected.

“If you loved someone . . .”

“Love is a myth,” he said harshly, “a fairy tale that mothers tell their children. My grandmother told me that my parents weren’t in love while they lived together. I was fond of my wife, but I had no more love for her than she had for me. If you want to know what I think of as love, Bernadette, it has more to do with bedrooms than wedding bands.”

She gasped and put her hand to her throat. “Eduardo!”

His eyebrows levered up. “Don’t you know what I’m talking about, or are you as green as you look?”

“You shouldn’t speak of such things to me!”

“Why not? You’re twenty.” His eyes narrowed. “Haven’t you ever felt the fires burn inside you with a man? Haven’t you ever wanted to know what happens in the dark between a man and a woman?”

“No!”

He smiled mockingly. “Then your father is truly hoping for a miracle if he means to wed you to European nobility. You will be expected to do your duty, of course. A man needs a son to inherit the title. Or didn’t that thought occur?”

"I can't . . . I won't . . . have a child!" she said, shaken.

"Then what use are you to a titled nobleman?"

"As much use as I am to my father," she agreed. "Absolutely none. But he won't stop matchmaking."

"Won't he?" His eyes averted to the horizon, thoughtfully. "Perhaps he will, after all."

"Don't tell me—you've come up with a way to save me!"

He chuckled. "I might have, at that." He studied her curiously. "But you might think you've given up the frying pan for the fire."

"How so?"

He put a hand on her thigh and watched her squirm and struggle to remove it.

"I want you," he said curtly. "An alliance between us could solve my problems and your own."

She colored. "You . . . want . . . *me*?"

"Yes." He caught her gloved hand in his and held it tightly. "You knew it that day in the parlor when we stared at each other so blatantly. You know it now. Perhaps it's a less than honorable reason for two people to marry—that you need saving from a cold marriage and I need saving from bankruptcy. But in my house, Bernadette, at least you'd be independent."

"And you would save your inheritance." She eyed him curiously. "You know that I'm the bookkeeper for our ranch, don't you, and that I can budget to the bone?"

He smiled slowly. "Maria sings your praises constantly. And even your father has to admit that you manage his affairs admirably." His black eyes narrowed. "Your quick mind with figures would be an asset to me as well, Bernadette. And the fact that I find you desirable is a bonus."

She watched him with renewed interest. "You didn't have to ask me this way," she said, thinking out loud. "You could have courted me and pretended to be in love with me to get me to marry you, and I'd never have known the difference."

"Yes, I could have," he agreed at once. "But I'd have known the difference. That's a low, vile thing for any man to do, even to save his livelihood." He let go of her hand. "I offer you an alliance of friends and a slaking of passions, when," he added wickedly, "you have the courage to invite me into your bed. There are advantages and disadvantages. Weigh them carefully and let me know what you decide. But decide soon," he added intently. "There isn't much time."

"I promise you, I'll think about it," she said, trying to suppress her delight.

He nodded. He smiled at her. "It might not be so bad," he mused. "I have a way with women, and you need someone to make you take care of yourself, as well as independence from your father. It could be a good marriage."

"I'd still be a bargain bride," she pointed out, despite her embarrassment at his bluntness.

"With a Spanish master," he murmured, and grinned. "But I promise to be patient."

She colored again. "You wicked man!"

"One day," he told her after he'd mounted his own horse, laughing softly, "you may be glad of that. Adiós, Bernadette!"

Chapter Four

Bernadette was over the moon about Eduardo's incredible proposition, but now she had to find a way to implement it. Her father wasn't even considering Eduardo anymore.

He still wanted a European nobleman for Bernadette, and he wasn't going to quit until he had one. She gave up worrying about it and concentrated on finding ways and means to marry herself to the man she loved—although he'd admitted that he didn't love her. Surely she loved him enough for both of them.

Meanwhile, her father's two candidates had arrived, bag and baggage, along with several members of prominent families who were staying with the Barrons until the ball. The Culhanes had backed out at the last minute, apologetic about having some problems close to home that had to be addressed. They sent their regrets, but everyone else showed up.

Bernadette was already having problems with the German nobleman. Klaus Branner liked the looks of Bernadette and he became her shadow. He was in his late forties, blond and paunchy and shorter than she. The Italian was volatile and found Bernadette not at all to his liking, so he spent most of his time with her father, talking about guns and hunting.

Bernadette resented having to fight off the advances of the German, but her father made it clear that he wasn't going to intervene.

"Eduardo doesn't want you, he's made that perfectly clear by his absence," her father said doggedly when she complained about the amorous duke. He made a helpless gesture with his hand and wouldn't look at her plaintive expression. "You'll get . . . used to it," he said stiffly, and went to rejoin his Italian friend.

But Bernadette didn't get used to it. And it got worse. One day, the day before the ball, in fact, the German duke maneuvered Bernadette behind the Chinese screen in the living room and put his pudgy hands on her breasts.

She kicked him in the shin hard enough to make him cry out, and then she ran for the safety of her locked bedroom, weeping copiously with rage and the horrible revulsion she felt.

No longer could she bear the disgusting advances of her prospective bridegroom. If her own father wouldn't defend her, there was nothing left to do except run away.

She dressed in her riding habit and boots, drew

a blanket from the dresser, and went out the window of her room. Casting a watchful eye around, in case her pursuer was anywhere nearby, she eased into the kitchen where Maria was working on the noon meal.

"Niña!" Maria exclaimed when she confronted her mistress dressed for the trail and carrying a colorful serape. "What are you up to?"

"Pack me something to eat, and very quickly, please. I'm running away," she said firmly.

Maria's black eyebrows lifted. "But you cannot! Not alone! Please, speak to your father!"

"I did speak to him," she said through trembling lips. "He said I'd get used to having that repulsive Branner man fondle me! I won't, I tell you! He's put his pudgy hands on me for the last time! I'm leaving!"

"But it is so dangerous!"

"Staying here is more dangerous," Bernadette said. "I will not be harrassed and treated like a woman of the streets by that horrible man while my father stands by and does nothing! If I don't go, I'll shoot him! Please pack me something to eat, and hurry, Maria, before they catch me!"

Maria mumbled worriedly in Spanish, but she did as she was asked, wrapping a piece of cold chicken and a hunk of bread, all that was left from the last meal, in a cloth and stuffing them into a saddlebag, along with a jar of canned peaches. "So little. You will starve long before night falls."

"Don't worry, I'll be much safer among the snakes and cactus than I will here with that German octopus!" Bernadette hugged Maria affectionately and cautiously crossed to the stable. She made the confused stable boy saddle her horse, looking around warily for anyone who might want to stop her.

Once she was in the saddle, she headed quickly for the nearby mountains, where she could hide in safety. She had no gun, but hopefully she wouldn't need one. If she could hide out for two or three days, just long enough to frighten her father, she might get her point across. Public opinion would not be favorable to a man who sent his unhappy daughter running into the wilds of Texas to escape an unwanted suitor!

She rode until the skies began to go purple and red in late afternoon, then she stopped her mount by a small stream under some trees and unsaddled her horse, careful to tether him so that he wouldn't wander during the night.

She did know how to build a campfire, and it was a necessary skill here in the desert country where nights could be freezing. She used her saddle for a pillow and the saddle blanket for a bed, with her colorful serape for cover. It was going to be a very uncomfortable night, but she could bear it. Anything was preferable to having that repulsive man pawing her!

But if it was easy to contemplate a night in the desert, it was harder to endure it. She knew that bandits often raided isolated camps. She had no money, but she was easily recognizable to people in the area as the daughter of its most wealthy local citizen. She could be kidnapped and held for ransom—or worse. She shivered at the thought of dirty, greedy hands on her body.

She sat looking into the flames, shivering, and wondering where her mind had been for her to consider such a reckless plan of action. She jumped at every noise she heard. It was the first time she'd ever been completely alone in her life, and it was unnerving as she sat and thought of all the things that could happen to her because of her folly. The very worst was considering what might happen to her if she had an attack out here, in the middle of nowhere. She had nothing to stop one, not even coffee.

She thought of Eduardo and what he'd said to her, about the two of them conspiring to arrange their own marriage. It was the best chance she had to escape her father's plans for her. But it frightened her a little to think of Eduardo intimately. He would need a son. It seemed to be almost a mania with men. What if she could never steel herself to sleep with him? Would he still be willing to marry her, with that threat hanging over them?

* * *

While she was sitting alone in the desert by her campfire, freezing under the light blanket and deliberating about her misery, something quite different was going on back at the ranch.

Eduardo had arrived, intending to see Colston Barron and put the proposition of marrying Bernadette to him one more time. If the man refused, he could simply elope with his intended bride. Possession was, after all, nine-tenths of the law, and Bernadette was willing.

The ranch owner was in his study with a slight, dark man and a heavyset older one, and they were examining a fowling piece when Eduardo was shown in by Maria.

"Well, Eduardo!" Colston said, nonplussed. "I wasn't expecting you. You haven't been to see us in such a long time that I thought you'd put us right out of your life, lad!"

Eduardo glanced at the small, younger man and then at the German with barely concealed contempt. Having had a brief conversation with Maria already, he was infuriated by Colston's lack of action on Bernadette's behalf.

"I came to ask a question, but it can wait. Are you aware," Eduardo continued in a cold, quiet tone, "that Bernadette has run away?"

The little Irishman's eyes almost popped out of his round face. "She's . . . what?"

"Run away," Eduardo repeated. "Maria says

she's been gone for the better part of an hour. Didn't you *know*?"

Colston colored. "Well, no."

"And I suppose her reason is as vague to you as her absence?" he added, glaring daggers at the German nobleman, who colored with embarrassment.

Colston cleared his throat. "Never mind that. Where do you think she's gone?"

"Probably to the mountains," Eduardo said through his teeth. "And a rancher nearby has just had cattle stolen by a group of outlaws. It is not a good time for Bernadette to be alone and unprotected, especially in her weakened physical condition!"

Colston felt like going through the floor. His inadequacies were being paraded like horses before his honored guests. His fists clenched. "I'll have one of my men go and look for her at once," he said.

"You'll do nothing of the sort!" Eduardo returned, his temper aroused and evident. "If you don't care enough to look for her yourself, don't bother. I'll find her and bring her back!"

Colston wavered between relief and indignation. "I appreciate your help, lad, but my daughter is no concern of yours—"

"Or of yours, apparently." Eduardo's onyx eyes were snapping. "What a hell of a pity that a young woman can't escape being molested in her own home!"

"Now, see here!" Colston began.

"Who is this crude upstart?" the German demanded in his thickly accented English.

Eduardo moved toward him with a lithe, steady gait that was intimidating enough to make the shorter, more rotund foreign nobleman back up a step. "I'll tell you who I am," Eduardo said with ice dripping from every syllable. "I'm a friend of the family. And if you're still here when I bring Bernadette home, you'll wish you weren't."

With a final glare at Colston, he turned and strode angrily out the door.

Colston swallowed and then swallowed again. The Italian, who hadn't said a word, smiled ruefully.

"I think that your daughter will not marry either of us, signore," the Italian mused, "if that man has his way."

"I no longer wish to marry her," Herr Branner said gruffly, scrambling to save his wounded ego. "She is cold. She has no spark. Such a woman would drive a man mad." He bowed to Colston formally. "If you will provide a buggy and one of your men to drive me to the station, Herr Barron, I will make my departure. Sadly, I must tell you that I cannot remain for your ball."

He clicked his heels and was gone before Colston could think of a word to say to stop him.

"Since I have no wish to marry your daughter, either, I might as well go with him," Maretti said with a chuckle. "I would enjoy the ball, but not under the circumstances. May I extend my congratulations and my condolences to you on your daughter's forthcoming marriage. I believe you will find your prospective son-in-law something of a trial."

Colston's only consolation was that Eduardo had connections to European royalty, and the man had been, after all, his first choice. It amazed him that Eduardo should deliberately stay away for weeks and then suddenly arrive at the worst possible time. On the other hand, his vehemence on Bernadette's behalf was quite encouraging. All might not be lost.

At least Eduardo would find the girl; Colston had no doubt of that. But he dreaded the reappearance of the two of them.

Eduardo rode out toward the distant mountains, still smoldering at Bernadette's father's callous attitude toward her. What sort of father would leave his daughter wide open to unwanted advances from a houseguest, regardless of the reason? He hated the very thought of another man's hands on Bernadette.

He tracked her to the mountains and then had to slow his pace as her trail became more difficult to follow. He heard a sound that chilled his blood—the scream of a puma. That was another danger that Bernadette probably hadn't thought of, and he was certain that she wasn't armed. He always wore a sidearm and carried a rifle. He hoped he wouldn't need them.

As darkness began to fall in earnest, he worried that he might not find her in time to spare her a terrifying night alone in the desert. The night air wouldn't be good for her weak lungs, and few people realized how cold it became after the sun set. He always carried two blankets in his saddle pack, just in case.

He was so frustrated that he almost missed the faint smell of smoke. Then, when a whiff of burning wood came to him, his heart leapt. He dismounted and climbed up on a boulder to get a better look in the direction from which he believed the smoke came. Sure enough, he spotted a small campfire down below.

It was precarious going down the slope in the dark, but his gelding was surefooted and careful, and he took his time.

As he rode into the small circle of light the campfire provided, Bernadette jumped to her feet with a blanket around her and stood shivering as she waited for him to come close enough to see.

She lifted her chin. "You'd better not come any closer," she called hoarsely. "My father and brothers are just outside the camp. They'll hear me if I scream!"

He chuckled at her nerve. She looked fragile and vulnerable, but what spirit, even in the face of tangible danger!

"You never cease to amaze me," he said gently as he rode near enough for her to recognize him.

"Eduardo!" She ran toward him when he dismounted, looking up into his dark face with absolute trust and relief.

He smiled, discarding his gloves to catch her hands in his. "You're freezing! Didn't you have another blanket?"

"Only this one." Her teeth chattered. "I didn't realize it got quite this cold. Why are you here?" she added worriedly. "Did my father send you?"

His face hardened. "Maria told me what happened. I came to find you."

"You, not my father," she murmured sadly.

"He was going to send one of his ranch hands. I told him not to bother."

"He should have sent one of his candidates for my bridegroom instead," she said coldly.

"I believe the German will be on the first train north," he said dryly. "And the other gentleman probably won't be far behind him."

"Oh, thank God!"

He retrieved his blankets from his saddle pack and wrapped one around her before he removed the saddlebags and began to make coffee in a small pot.

"What did the German do to you, Bernadette?"

he asked when he had the coffeepot on the fire and they were both sitting nearby.

She averted her embarrassed eyes in the bright light of the campfire. "Never mind. It doesn't matter, if he's gone."

"It does matter! I should have shot the—"

"It's all right," she interrupted before he could voice the curse. "I can't be the first woman who was ever fondled against her will."

He looked furious. He watched her move away from the campfire and ease down onto her makeshift bed. "Were you planning to stay the night?"

She nodded. "I thought if I frightened my father enough, he might cancel his plans."

"He'll cancel them now," he assured her, holding his hands to the fire. "I promise you he will."

She let out a long sigh. "Thank you for coming to find me."

He glanced at her curiously. "You might not consider yourself saved when I tell you what I have in mind."

Her eyebrows lifted. "What?"

"I intend to keep you out all night."

He expected shock and fear. But after a minute's hesitation, she laughed delightedly. "What a wonderful idea! If his prospective bridegrooms haven't left, they certainly will after this!"

"I intend to displace them," he said shortly. "If your father wants a noble for a son-in-law, he can have me. I'll take a damned sight better care of you than he does, and I won't drag you off to Europe to die."

She stared at him with delight. "You really want to marry me?"

He nodded. "It won't be a love match," he said, his voice quiet and calming, "but you'll have freedom and independence, and I'll take care of you."

"I'll take care of you, too," she replied gently.

He was shocked to discover that he liked the idea of someone taking care of him. It wasn't acceptable to admit it, of course, and he wasn't going to. But it touched him as few things in his recent past had.

"Have you eaten anything?" he asked.

She laughed, pulling her blanket closer. "I had a roll and some cold chicken that Maria packed for me, but nonetheless, I'm hungry," she said simply.

"So am I."

"I don't suppose you brought anything to eat?"

He chuckled. "I came in rather a hurry," he said. "But I stopped by Mrs. Brown's café on the way here and had her pack some cold meat and bread and cheese." He shook his head as he retrieved it from the saddlebag. "I must have had a premonition."

"What a lovely provider you're going to make!" she exclaimed.

He put cold roast beef and cheese on a thick

slice of bread and handed it to her. She ate hungrily, amazed that her misery should have turned to such pleasure. Eduardo might not love her, but he was offering her a new start, a future that would free her from her father's attempted domination and manipulation. Gone was the spectre of a foreign marriage, of having to go to live in another country.

"Counting your regrets?" he asked a few minutes later, having noticed her studious demeanor.

Her head came up quickly, and she shook it. "Oh, no," she said at once. "I was counting my blessings! It will be so nice not to have to depend on my father for my living."

He frowned slightly. "It won't be a life of leisure," he cautioned.

"I can cook," she replied calmly. "And sew and clean, and I can certainly keep books and budget! I'm not totally an invalid, and I imagine that I shall be much healthier if I am also happy."

"That may be so." He poured coffee into one of two tin cups he'd retrieved from his saddlebag and handed it to her. "Drink that," he said. "It will help to warm you, and it may ward off what I fear is an unavoidable reaction to being chilled."

She grimaced as she took a sip. "I'm sorry," she said. "I hadn't planned to do this until Herr Branner got amorous behind the Chinese screen." She looked up. "You don't have a Chinese screen, do you?"

He grinned wickedly. "No. But I'll buy you one when we make our fortune, if you like."

She shivered blatantly. "No, thank you."

"You'll be safe from foreign suitors with me, at least," he said, sobering. "And I won't blame you for things over which you have no control."

"You mean my mother, don't you?" she asked perceptively. He nodded. "I'm sorry my father can't give up her memory. He might have remarried and been very happy, but there was no talking to him about it. He mourns her as if she died yesterday, and blames me for her death."

"Perhaps he blames himself, Bernadette," he said quietly, "and takes it out on you."

She pulled the blanket closer. The chill was worse now, rippling through her slender body like a blow. "It's so c-cold!"

He put down his cup and joined her on the bedroll. "You mustn't take a chill. Forgive me, Bernadette, I mean no insult, but I have no other means of warming you."

He drew her down onto the bedroll spread and into his arms, smiling when she stiffened. "Yes, I know, it's going to be very intimate," he said, wrapping the blanket closer around her shoulders as he eased both of them back against the saddle she'd used for a pillow. "You'll get used to it."

She giggled nervously. "That's what my father said, about the pudgy little man touching me."

He stiffened then, his eyes glittering with anger.

"No woman should ever have to get used to something she finds offensive."

She laid her cheek against his broad chest with a little sigh and closed her eyes. Bit by bit, she forced her taut muscles to relax. As she did, she felt the warmth of him radiating around her.

"Oh, this is so much better," she whispered. "Thank you!"

He chuckled, drawing her closer. "Shameless hussy," he murmured. "You should be screaming for assistance."

"I don't need assistance. You're going to marry me."

"Yes, I am." He stretched his strained muscles and laid back against the saddle. "It will have to be an event," he added. "We can't run away and get married, as Queen Isabella and King Ferdinand did, without their parents' knowledge or consent."

"What?" She opened her eyes and looked up at him. "The king and queen of Spain eloped?"

He smiled. "Indeed. From what we are told, it was Isabella's idea. She was barely out of her teens. She had Ferdinand meet her secretly and she put the proposal to him that they would marry and unite his native kingdom of Aragon with hers of Castile. From such an alliance, they would conquer and rule all of Spain."

"And he agreed?"

"Yes. They married in secret and went back to their respective kingdoms. At the death of Ferdinand's father, when he became king of Aragon, they announced their marriage to the world and joined forces to drive the Moors out of Spain. Think how much they accomplished—and all because a spirited young woman had the courage to change history." He looked down at her fondly. "She must have been like you, I think, Bernadette. You were never one to stand meekly by and let others decide your fate. No simpering young miss would be lying alone with a man in the dark, defying her father and the rest of the world."

"Oh, I'm not so brave," she protested. "It was selfish. I didn't want to be a human sacrifice."

His arm contracted. "Neither will you be. But back to the matter of marriage. There will be a scandal, you understand."

"Yes. I've just been ruined," she agreed easily.

He glared at her. "Ruined?"

She peered up at him with a wicked little smile. "Compromised? Ravished? Seduced?"

He didn't smile. He was registering the softness of her in his arms, the spark of joy it gave him to hold her so tightly. "Seduced?" he asked softly, and drew her closer. "What an excellent idea!"

Chapter Five

BERNADETTE WAS VERY BRAVE UNTIL EDUARDO GENTLY eased her flat onto the bedroll and loomed over her with intent.

Her heart raced like mad, and her breathing, already dicey, was strained and audible.

He relented at once. His hand came up to brush back the wisps of blond hair that had escaped from the neat bun atop her head.

"Forgive me," he said softly. "I only meant to tease, not to frighten you. Breathe slowly, Bernadette, slowly. There's nothing to be afraid of."

She fought to relax, to repress the furious beating of her heart. Her hand went to her throat and rested there while she looked up at him with wide, tortured eyes.

"Shall I get up and make some more coffee?" he asked. "Will it help you to breathe more easily?"

She shook her head. "It's not the asthma," she whispered.

He stilled. "Then what?"

She bit her lower lip. Her eyes searched his. "It's being so close to you," she admitted shyly, and lowered her gaze to his mouth.

"Ah."

Only a soft syllable, but it electrified her senses. She couldn't contain her nervousness. Her fingers went to the front of his shirt and pressed there. Her courage seemed to desert her when she needed it most.

"It excites me, too, amada," he said at her lips, watching them part helplessly. He leaned closer. Around them the darkness was like a blanket, the dying fire giving even more intimacy to their situation. "Kiss me," he said on a breath.

She felt his lips touch hers, brush them. It was a tender, whispery caress, but it made her whole body go rigid with unexpected pleasure. She gasped and her small hands caught at his jacket and bit into it as she clung, trying to coax him down to her. While his mouth teased her lips, his lean fingers moved up her ribcage and paused at the thrust of her breasts. He suddenly felt her body jerk.

His thumbs edged out gently, teasing. "Will you accept my hands?" he whispered. "Or is such intimacy with me unwelcome to you?"

She couldn't speak for the turmoil inside her. She shivered and her body arched just slightly. He understood the silent message.

He sighed as his fingers smoothed over the part

of her that had known only two such caresses. But this one wasn't repulsive. It was glorious. She relaxed into the bedroll and looked up at him with soft, dazed eyes as he touched her. He felt her nipples go hard under his hands and he smiled gently, reassuringly. "You aren't afraid of me."

"No," she whispered breathlessly. She touched his face, his hard mouth, letting him see the excitement in her eyes. She gasped as his fingers became more insistent. He held the small hardness between his thumb and forefinger and tested its firmness boldly. There was a look on his dark, lean face that she'd never seen before. It was intent, sensual, totally absorbed.

"Is this what men and women do together in the darkness?" she whispered curiously.

"Yes," he replied softly. "But without clothing, amada."

She was embarrassed at her own frankness, much less his. But they were to be married. She had to come to grips with her nameless fears.

"And what then?" she asked.

The sound of his hands moving on the fabric of her dress was loud in the soft darkness, which was broken only by the crackling of the fire and the distant sounds of night.

"Do you know anything of true intimacy?" he asked quietly.

"Only that men are made differently from women," she said. "One of the girls at my school had been with a man, though," she added shyly. "She said that it was very shocking and fun, and that their bodies became part of each other. None of us understood what she meant."

He searched her flushed face. "Do you want me to tell you, to explain what happens?"

"I think you must," she began. "If we are to be married."

"There is no doubt of that," he said solemnly. "I would never have touched you in this manner had my intentions been less than honorable. You're very innocent, Bernadette," he added, as if it disturbed him.

"And very nervous," she laughed shakily. "But I like the way it feels when you touch me."

"As do I."

He caught one of her small hands and drew it slowly to his belly, sliding it down until it encountered something unexpected and quite shocking. He controlled her instinctive withdrawal and held her hand there.

"This is where we are most different," he said softly. "This part of my body enters yours where you are most a woman. We join and in this manner we pleasure each other in a secret way."

Her shocked outcry was audible.

"What a disservice our parents do us by keeping such things mysterious," he said, his voice deep and solemn. "By surrounding them with myth and romance. Sexual intimacy is a gift from God,

Bernadette, not a shameful thing, but a reverent thing between man and wife. It serves not only to give us the greatest pleasure life can offer, but also to create children."

She cleared her throat, embarrassed by so much blunt speech about a subject that all her life had been clouded and hazy. "Nobody ever talks about it," she said.

"Such subjects, they say, are unfit and indecent for discussion between men and women." He chuckled softly. "But I'm a wicked man, Bernadette, and you're no shrinking violet, despite your frail lungs."

Her hand was still resting where his had put it, but now he began to feel familiar to her, less shocking. She was about to say so when her fingers moved restlessly and something began to happen to him, something tangible.

She heard a deep sound in his throat, accompanied by the sudden jerk of his body.

Fascinated, she looked into his eyes as he became aroused and she felt it happen under her trembling hand.

"Another aspect of the mystery revealed," he said in a lighthearted but strained tone.

She was awed. She felt suddenly old, wise. Her eyes searched his without embarrassment. She swallowed. Her body felt the wonder of what they were sharing, her mind rippling with forbidden thoughts. Her own boldness surprised her as her fingers moved hesitantly.

He stilled them at once with a husky laugh. "Curiosity is dangerous," he whispered to her. "Especially in a situation such as ours. These explorations are best saved for marriage."

She smiled shyly. "I look forward to them."

"So do I." He rolled over onto his back, grimacing a little because he was aroused and uncomfortable. But he pulled her close to his side and covered her more tightly with the blanket. "You are unexpected."

"Brazen?" she murmured.

His arm contracted. "A delightful surprise," he replied. "The only married intimacy I have known was distasteful and demeaning."

"What?"

He sighed. "Do you know how Consuela reacted to me when I took her, Bernadette? She stiffened her entire body, gritted her teeth, closed her eyes, and mumbled prayers until I was done. After the second time, I never visited her bed again. Our son was born nine months later, and I knew there could never be another child after him. My pride would not have survived another night in her bed."

She bit her lip. "Oh, dear."

"Oh, dear?" he echoed, curious.

"What if . . . what if I'm like that?"

He laughed softly. "You won't be."

"How can we know for sure, until . . ."

He moved just a little, tugged the blanket down to her waist, and suddenly put his mouth right over one small breast.

It was the most incredible sensation she'd ever felt. She cried out with pure delight, her hands catching his dark head and cradling it to her, pulling at it as her body arched to keep the forbidden contact.

He was laughing! She felt his breath against the moist fabric as he bent again and took the hard nipple in his teeth and nibbled it with exquisite tenderness until she shivered.

He lifted his head, keeping one warm hand over the place he'd kissed as he looked down into her wide eyes. "I know that you are not and never will be like Consuela," he whispered.

She searched his face. "You truly are wicked."

He smiled. "Yes. Aren't you glad?"

She hid her face against him and smiled as he folded her close and brought the blanket back over them. She was glad, but it wouldn't do to admit it. Marriage, it seemed, wasn't going to be anything of the terror she'd expected.

But when they awoke the next morning, she was embarrassed and a little shy with Eduardo. He noticed this and held her when she would have jumped up from their shared bedroll.

"Nothing has changed since last night," he

chided softly. “Except, of course, that you are now ‘ruined’ and must marry me.”

She sighed. “Yes, I know. And we'll never live it down, not for the rest of our lives.”

“You must admit, it was the only way to secure your father's permission,” he reminded her. “And to save you from his own candidates.”

She lay back against the saddle, forlorn and worried. “He would have given it, gladly, but you didn't come near me. He assumed that you didn't want me.”

His breath caught. “He said nothing! Nor did you!”

She shifted a little away from him. “You were his best candidate from the beginning, I think,” she said. “He offered you as an alternative to the German and the Italian and said that if I could interest you in his proposal, he'd send the foreigners home. But you didn't come, so he assumed that you weren't interested in me at all.”

“We spoke the day of your asthma attack,” he said shortly. “I told him then that I would not be averse to marrying you.”

She gasped. “He said nothing!”

He took one of her small hands in his and held it lightly. “I was ashamed of my own behavior,” he said curtly. “It was dishonest and low to arrange such a marriage behind your back, without your knowledge. My conscience ate at me like acid.”

Her heart skipped with pure delight. He wasn't

such a rogue after all. But it surprised her that he'd been willing to marry her.

"You might have said something to me about it," she said.

He chuckled. "Yes, I might have." He turned his head and suddenly rolled over, so that her face was beneath his. "But I was very attracted to you, and not at all certain that I wanted such a complication."

Her thin eyebrows rose. "You wanted a wife who didn't attract you?"

He shrugged. "Put like that, it sounds absurd."

"I think I understand, a little," she replied. Her gaze was intent on his handsome face. "You wanted to be honest about how you felt. You weren't willing to pretend an emotion you didn't feel."

He nodded. "That was it exactly, Bernadette."

"So you stayed away and my father thought you'd decided against marrying me at all."

"And I thought that he'd decided I wasn't good enough to marry his daughter," he confessed.

Her eyebrows arched. "You didn't!"

"I did."

She shook her head. "But, didn't you know that he admires you more than any other man he knows?"

He sighed. "No. I didn't." He searched her soft eyes. Impulsively, his fingers went to her eyebrows and traced them curiously. "I'm half Spanish and half Texan," he said. "It's a curious mixture, like being part Indian. Some people object. They call me a half-breed."

"Are there Indians in your past?" she asked.

"If there are, my grandmother would never admit it." He searched her eyes a little worriedly. "You're going to have a hard time with her, Bernadette. She won't approve of my marrying outside the nobility, despite my mixed parentage."

"It isn't as if we're different races," she pointed out.

"And your father is wealthy. I know that. But it won't matter to her. She's old-fashioned about such things. Like your father," he added curtly, "bloodlines matter too much to her."

"My father said that she might not be able to find you another match in Spain."

His eyes flashed. "Because my wife died under mysterious circumstances," he added for her.

She reached up and touched his hard, thin mouth. "Don't be angry. We can't have secrets, not in a marriage such as ours is to be."

He grimaced. His fingers caught hers and held them. "No, we can't. But those secrets are for a time when you and I are less constrained with each other." His fingers contracted on hers. "I didn't kill Consuela," he said. "That will have to do for now."

"Your grandmother is to come this summer, isn't she?"

"She'll come the minute she knows there's to be a wedding, and she'll bring Lupe with her."

That was a new name. "Lupe?"

"Lupe de Rias," he said shortly.

"A man or a woman?"

"A woman. And my grandmother's first choice of wives for me, after Consuela."

Bernadette's heart skipped. "You mean, there is a candidate to marry you, one of the nobility?"

He looked hunted. His dark eyes went to Bernadette's breasts and he remembered the soft warmth of them under his mouth. They weren't large at all, but they were pert and firm and sweet to touch. He wished he could see them through the fabric.

"What?" he asked, distracted.

"I said, you haven't lost your chance to marry into the nobility?"

"I don't want Lupe," he said simply. "I prefer you."

Her heart jumped and she laughed softly. "Do you, really, pitiful lungs and all?"

"Yes." His head bent and his mouth found her soft breast.

She gasped and caught his face in her hands, but it was a halfhearted effort to restrain him.

"I want to look at you," he murmured. His hands moved on her body and his face shifted to her soft neck, her cheek, her lips. He moved, so that one long leg smoothed sensually over both of hers.

His mouth covered hers and her hands clenched at his neck while she fought for a little sanity. She didn't find it. Her lips opened, as he'd taught them to the night before, and she reveled in the slow caress of his fingers.

He lifted his head to look at her rapt face and misty eyes. His hand covered her breast blatantly. "I would sooner cut off my leg than trade you for Lupe," he said huskily. "Already you belong to me."

She relaxed into the bedroll and stared at him hungrily, her body yielded, soft, patently enjoying his bold caresses.

He sighed heavily and glanced around them. "The day is getting away from us already," he said regretfully and drew his hands away from her. "As much as I prefer to stay here and continue this delightful pastime, we have to face the music." He stood up and pulled her up with him, pausing to smooth back her disheveled hair. "You need a brush, and I haven't one."

She smiled. "It won't matter. We're in so much trouble already that my father probably won't even notice." She grimaced. "He's going to be furious."

"Do you think so?" He bent and kissed the tip of her nose. "I don't think he will be, Bernadette."

"Eduardo."

He put a finger over her soft mouth. His eyes went down to her bodice and lingered there while he smiled wickedly. "I hope the heat will dry that swiftly," he gestured, "long before your father sees it."

She looked down at the small wet spot just over her nipple and she laughed shyly. "It will," she said.

He held her by the shoulders, his face dark and quiet and very mature. "You delight me," he said softly. "Your responses are everything a man could hope for, dream of. We'll make a good marriage, Bernadette."

"Yes, I think we will," she agreed. She hesitated. "You don't love me, though."

He hesitated, too. He didn't want to be this honest with her, but perhaps it was the wisest way. "No," he confessed. "I'm fond of you. I like your spirit. I love the way it makes me feel when I make love to you. When the children come, they'll bind us even closer. It will be enough."

She didn't know about that. She loved him desperately. And there was that remark about children. She was still terrified of childbirth, even though she felt the same overwhelming desire that he did.

"Stop worrying," he said when he saw her brooding expression. "Trust me. Everything's going to be all right."

"I do hope so," she said.

He smiled. "Wait and see."

It took them an hour to get home. Sure enough, as Bernadette had feared, Colston Barron was pacing the area near the stable, smoking a cigar and looking ferocious. He glared at both of them without saying a word while they dismounted and turned over their horses to the boy to stable.

Eduardo took Bernadette's cold little hand in his and held it tightly as they approached her father, but he wasn't looking apologetic. In fact, he almost swaggered.

"I'm sending a cable to my grandmother today, to announce my forthcoming marriage to Bernadette," he said, spiking the little Irishman's guns before he could get the cigar out of his mouth. He held up a hand when Colston started to speak. "There will be protocol to observe, of course, and our relatives will have to have time to make arrangements to attend. My best friend belongs to the House of Windsor, and I would like him to stand with me at the ceremony. You do understand that it will be a gala event, I hope," he added with deliberate hauteur, "since Bernadette will be marrying into most of the royal houses of Europe."

Colston looked as if he might swoon. "You mean, you still want to marry her?!"

"Of course I want to marry her. I always did. We get along well together. It will be a good marriage."

Colston wiped his sweaty brow, looking from one to the other. His face hardened a little. "But she didn't come home last night, and the servants all know it." He groaned. "They'll gossip."

"Not when they know that she spent the night with my cousin Carlita from Mexico City, who was staying with me overnight," he replied calmly. He let go of Bernadette's hand and lit a cigar of his own. "I have brought her home this morning. My servants will swear, of course, that this is the truth."

Colston let out a long sigh. "It's all my fault," he said miserably. "I thought you didn't want her anymore. The German seemed to." He shifted uncomfortably, avoiding his daughter's accusing eyes. "I thought she'd get used to him. I never dreamed she'd run away." He glared at Bernadette. "You could have been eaten by wolves, you silly twit!"

"Don't you call me a twit!" she shot right back. "Who was it who told me to let that horrible little man do what he liked, all because you wanted a noble son-in-law?"

"Whist, and don't you be talking to me in such a manner!"

Eduardo stepped between them when he heard Bernadette's breath begin to rasp. "Arguing about an accomplished fact is a waste of effort," he said calmly. "We have a wedding to arrange. My cousin

Lupe is coming along with my grandmother to visit. She arranged a wedding for the Spanish royal house just recently and is familiar with protocol and tradition. She will take care of the details."

"And I'll pay for them," Colston said at once. He looked relieved yet guilty. He stared at Bernadette as if he were looking for signs of upheaval. "In two months, you said," he added worriedly with a pointed glance at Bernadette's slender waist.

"How dare you!" Eduardo burst out furiously when he saw the speculative gaze.

Colston sucked in his breath. "My boy, I didn't say a word!"

"She was upset, alone, hungry, and frightened—chilled into the bargain! Even a scoundrel would hesitate to accost a woman in such a condition, least of all any decent man!"

"I apologize, yes, I do," Colston said at once. "You must forgive an old man's suspicions. I know better."

"Yes, you do," Eduardo said, a little less ruffled. He stared down at Bernadette. "I assume that the ball hasn't been cancelled?" he asked suddenly.

"Well, no," Colston began hesitantly. "I wasn't certain what to do when she didn't come home," he added stiffly. "I didn't know you'd even found her. Anything could have happened. I was just about to call my guests together and make arrangements to send them home."

"Unnecessary," Eduardo replied. "Do you have a gown?" he asked Bernadette.

She smiled. "Yes. Papa sent me to town. It's a Paris original."

"The color?"

"It's white," she told him. "With pink silk roses and tiny blue bows."

"How very appropriate," he murmured. "The Ramirez betrothal bracelet is emerald-studded gold. And the ring is a single emerald stone, very old. I will give them to you tonight, at the ball." He lifted her small hand in his and brought it softly to his mouth, kissing it warmly. "Until later, querida."

Chapter Six

WITH MATCHING EXPRESSIONS, BERNADETTE AND her father watched Eduardo ride off. Neither spoke for a minute.

"I thought he wanted nothing to do with marriage to you," Colston said stiffly.

She smiled to herself. "So did I." She turned and stared at her father curiously. "He thought you'd decided he wasn't good enough for me."

"No!" he burst out, horrified. "Surely not!"

She relented when she saw the worry on his face. "It's all right, Father. I told him that you never thought any such thing, and that you had a high regard for him."

"Sure and that's a relief," he said, dragging out a handkerchief to wipe his sweaty brow. He glanced at his daughter. "He stayed away. I thought he was telling us in a nice way that he'd changed his mind about you."

"Eduardo would never have done it in that way," she said, mildly surprised. "He'd have come to you and told you, if he had changed his mind."

"I suppose he would, at that." He put his hands behind him and clasped them as they walked. "How did the talk of marriage come about, then?"

"We were talking about the foreign visitors. He was angry that I ran away," she added, without saying why. "He said that if I have to marry a title, it can be his. He needs a loan and you need a titled son-in-law. This way, you both get what you want."

His small eyes narrowed. "So we would. But what do you get out of it?" he asked suspiciously.

"What I want most in the world," she said simply.

"And that is . . . ?"

"Eduardo," she replied with soft dignity. She turned toward the house.

He actually chuckled. "Whist, and isn't that a story, when you've been like worst enemies for years! What happened out there?" he asked after a minute.

"Nothing very dramatic, I'm afraid," she lied with a straight face. "He saved me from freezing. Maybe from dying. It was very cold and I hadn't packed enough blankets." She laughed. "He brought some." She didn't add that they'd shared them.

He looked different, almost guilty, and he wouldn't meet her eyes. "Herr Branner and Signore Maretti left for the train depot shortly after you ran for the hills." He stiffened a little. "I very much regret Herr Branner's behavior. But he did seem interested in you, and Eduardo didn't. But as God is my witness, girl, I never expected you to do something that dangerous and foolish." He glanced at her and away again. "I hope you know that I'd much rather have Eduardo for a son-in-law. I respect him. He was rather formidable when he came to your rescue." His features brightened. "By heaven, he was." He chuckled, lapsing back into the familiar brogue. "Bristling with fury, and steam coming from his ears, he was. I never expected him to blow up like that on your behalf, girl. I suppose it's not just my money that he wants, after all."

She smiled shyly. "I think he does like me . . . a little. It's no love match, as he says, but we have things in common." Her gaze fell to the ground. "We'll get by."

Her father shortened his strides and sighed. "I know it isn't precisely what you want, girl, a loveless match. But sometimes we have to settle for what we can get. Not all of us are lucky enough to find a love like I had with your mother."

His face hardened as he said it, and Bernadette knew that the truce was over. She lifted her long skirts and, calling a brief good-bye, lit out for the kitchen and the safety of Maria's company.

Maria was over the moon about the news.

"Oh, so furious, was el conde," she enthused as she cleared a space on the table for the platter of meat she'd just cooked. "He stalked in here after he spoke with your father and the foreign gentlemen and when he saw that nothing was left from our meal, he said that he would go to town and get food to carry with him, because he knew you would be as hungry as you would be cold."

"I was, despite what I took with me," Bernadette said. She blushed. "I didn't mean to cause so much trouble. I was very upset."

"And so was el conde," Maria added with a grin that showed her perfect white teeth. "Then, when you did not come home all night," she added, "your father became very stiff and worried." She shrugged. "I, of course, knew that the proprieties would be observed, whatever the situation. El conde is a gentleman, a man of quality. He would do nothing to stain your reputation."

"He didn't," she agreed. "But it wouldn't do for anyone to know that we were alone last night, so he is telling everyone that he took me to his home to stay with a cousin of his with whom I am friendly. This morning he brought me home."

Maria grinned. "A lovely tale. And of course, no one will doubt it!"

So much for that optimism, Bernadette thought later, when she was standing at the doorway of the ballroom in her lovely new dress and dozens of shrewd eyes watched her with suspicion and faint contempt.

She stood beside her father, watching him fidget. His face was red and he looked completely out of sorts. Bernadette thought he was angry at her until she saw him glance at her with mingled concern and apology.

"There's a scandal unfolding. That damned stable boy overheard us talking this morning," Colston said through his teeth. "He told a vaquero, who shared it with his relatives. Another of them was relating it yet again when one of our visitors who speaks Spanish overheard. He told everyone else. They all know that you were out with Eduardo all night. I'm sorry, girl."

She went red. Her impulsive behavior had destroyed her reputation. Eduardo might marry her, she might become respectable, but no one would forget that she'd stayed out all night with a man to whom she wasn't married.

"You hold your head up!" Colston said sharply when he saw her morose expression. "Sure and you've nothing to be ashamed of. Don't you let them look down at you! You're a Barron. You're as good as anyone here!"

She wasn't, and he knew it, but it was the first time he'd defended her in recent memory and it touched her.

"Thank you, Father," she said.

He looked uncomfortable again. His eyes went to the doorway and he seemed to slump with relief. "He's come, then."

She turned and saw Eduardo, elegant in evening clothes and looking every inch the nobleman. He walked straight to Bernadette, without pausing to speak to any of the guests, and his smile was for her alone.

"You look lovely," he told her, and lifted her hand very correctly to his lips. His head turned toward the assembled guests who were murmuring among themselves. He didn't have to be told that their secret was now public knowledge. He smiled mockingly at his host. "This would seem to be the best time to make the announcement," he told Colston. "Don't you agree?"

"Indeed I do, my boy." Colston walked to the band and requested silence. When he had the attention of his guests, he motioned Eduardo and Bernadette to join him. Eduardo gestured to his manservant hovering at the doorway with a velvet box in his hands.

"Ladies and gentlemen, I have an announcement to make! I wish to announce the betrothal of my daughter, Bernadette, to the Count Eduardo Rodrigo Ramirez y Cortes of Granada, Spain, and the Rancho Escondido of Valladolid County, Texas. I hope that all of you will join me in wishing the happy couple all the best for their future together!"

There was shocked hesitation, then lukewarm applause, and then a roar of applause.

Eduardo and Bernadette exchanged ironic

glances. He opened the velvet box his manservant was holding and withdrew a priceless antique gold-and-emerald bracelet which he clasped around Bernadette's small wrist. That was followed by the heirloom ring, also gold with emeralds. Amazingly, it fit her finger as if it had been made for it.

She looked up at Eduardo, who wore an expression of surprise.

"A good omen," he said for her ears alone. "It is said that the ring fits a Ramirez bride without adjustment if the match is a good one." He lifted her hand and kissed the ring.

Colston shook Eduardo's hand. His eyes were riveted to the jewelry Bernadette was now wearing. "I suppose you realize that she's wearing a king's ransom?" he asked softly. "Worth more than enough to restore your fortunes."

Eduardo looked at him levelly. "These two pieces are all I have left of my father's legacy," he said quietly. "They were handed down from the ancestor who had them created from Bolivian emeralds in the sixteenth century for his bride. They carry a curse, that whoever dares to sell them will lose not only his fortune, but his life." He smiled amusedly. "No one has ever had the nerve to test the curse."

"I see."

Bernadette was looking not at the jewels, but at Eduardo, her heart in her big, green eyes.

He looked down at her and saw her expression

and his breath caught. He knew, he'd always known, her feelings for him. But now there was a difference in the way he reacted to it. He felt himself shiver deep inside at the hunger that rose like a dry heat in his loins and spread over him like fire. He averted his eyes before the emotion could kindle a visible reaction that would embarrass them both.

There was more applause and the visitors gathered around to see Bernadette's ring and bracelet, no longer thinking of scandal when there was this juicy new bit of gossip to share with one another and take back to their homes.

"Why, this ring is magnificent!" Mrs. Carlisle said, grasping Bernadette's small hand in her pudgy fingers. "It must be worth a fortune!"

"It is," Eduardo replied, looking haughtily down at her. "But to discuss such matters in company is vulgar."

Turning red with embarrassment, she cleared her throat and put a hand to her fake pearls. Obviously her background and her experience as personal social secretary to one of the Astors had faded in the rough society of southwest Texas.

"Mrs. Carlisle made the arrangements for the ball," Bernadette said quickly, to save the poor woman any further embarrassment. "Didn't she do a lovely job?"

The older woman looked as if she might fall on Bernadette with relief.

"The motif is, indeed, elegant," Eduardo murmured.

Mrs. Carlisle's pride was restored. She smiled at Eduardo. "If you require any help with the wedding . . ." she began.

He held up a hand and smiled to soften the rejection. "You are most kind. However, my cousin Lupe will see to the arrangements."

Mrs. Carlisle looked concerned. "You do realize that even here a wedding of this sort will require a certain . . . elegance?"

He looked shocked. It went without saying that she was picturing a mariachi band and flamenco dancers. "My dear lady," he said with faint hauteur, "Lupe is a highborn Spanish noblewoman who only recently organized the marriage of the king's niece."

The woman was all but stuttering. Her opinion of Latin people was so evident as to be embarrassing, but it changed again, immediately. "The king . . . of Spain?"

"Of course."

"Then certainly she must know . . . must be quite adept . . . at such matters. You will excuse me? There is an old friend I must greet. Congratulations to you both!"

She was red-faced and all but running to escape putting her foot any farther into her mouth.

Eduardo watched her go with an elegantly raised eyebrow.

Bernadette's fingers nipped the back of his hand.

He chuckled as he grasped them tightly in his own. "Already you think to correct my bad behavior, wife-to-be?"

"She isn't as bad as I've made her out to be," she murmured with a grin.

He couldn't quite accept the change in Bernadette. They'd been adversaries for a long time, until just recently. Now she was so different that he wondered how they'd ever disagreed. She was poised and elegant and she looked lovely in the low-cut gown. He found himself remembering the softness of her breasts under his mouth, and he looked at them with pure pleasure. He hadn't yet tasted her soft skin. He wanted to. Badly.

She saw where his eyes were trained and brought up an elegant silk fan in a small gloved hand to block his gaze.

"Shame on you," she whispered.

He grinned. "Were you remembering as well?" he taunted softly.

She colored and looked quickly around to see if anyone had overheard.

"Don't you want to rap my fingers again?" he invited.

"You are going to make a very difficult husband," she said.

"Only from time to time. And never at night." He held up a hand when she looked near to an explosion. "There, there, I'll reform." He glanced around them. "Why were you the object of so much speculation when I arrived?"

"One of the vaqueros overheard us talking to my father this morning and told that we'd been out together all night. That dear soul told another," she said sarcastically. "Then another and another until, apparently, someone felt obliged to inform the rest of our visitors."

"Tell me the man's name and I'll have a little talk with him," he said, glancing around with danger in his eyes.

"I certainly won't," she replied, fanning herself. "You can't go around shooting people."

"Bernadette, you wound me!" He put his hand over his heart. "Would I be so uncivilized?"

"Of course you would," she replied without hesitation, snapping her fan shut to punctuate her words. "And my father would be horrified."

"I suppose he would." He caught her hand in his and drew her toward the dance floor. "I think they're all waiting for us to begin the waltz," he pointed out. He stopped in the middle of the ballroom and smiled down at her as his gloved hand insinuated itself around her small waist. "Are you up to this?" he asked gently. "Lungs not bothering you yet?"

She shook her head. "I suppose they should be, after the cold last night and all this perfume we're surrounded by. But I feel quite well." She smiled at him. "In fact, I feel as if I could float up to the ceiling."

He drew her just a little closer and as the band began to play a Strauss waltz, he pulled her into the first wide steps with expertise.

"We've never danced together," she said.

"I know. There never really was an opportunity. You dance very well."

"I was taught at finishing school. You dance well yourself." She let her feet carry her along to the rousing strains of the music, laughing softly with pleasure as they turned and floated together gracefully around the ballroom. "I suppose you learned as a boy," she said.

He nodded. "It was expected. All the social graces, languages, fencing."

"Can you really fence?" she asked, fascinated. "Could you teach me?"

He chuckled. "Why?"

"I've always wanted to learn. It's so beautiful to watch. I went to an exhibition in New York City when I was in school. It was so graceful."

"Your father would have a heart attack."

"My father doesn't have to know," she pointed out. "After all, you're not marrying him."

"No, I'm not." He searched her rapt features with more interest than ever. "What other accomplishments have you?"

"I can do needlepoint and knit and crochet," she

said. Her eyes danced. "And I can also ride a horse, shoot a rifle, and discuss politics."

"Useful skills in these parts," he murmured dryly. He whirled her around again and laughed as her eyes sparkled. "I like your hair that way," he said unexpectedly. "You should wear it down more often."

"At least one of our female guests thinks it's brazen and scandalous," she confided. "Like wearing pants!"

His gaze fell to her long skirts. "You can wear pants when we ride together, if you like, and shock every hand on the ranch."

She grinned. "Oh, Eduardo, it's going to be such fun being married!"

He was beginning to feel that way himself. It was unexpected. His first marriage had been dull and cold and unfeeling. Consuela had left him with scars that had never healed. But Bernadette was fiery and outrageous. She appealed to him as other women never had, and her innocence had a special appeal. He was glad that he'd started off right with her. He could never have courted her with false passion or pretended love. It was better to have their feelings for each other out in the open. That way, they could deal honestly with whatever difficulties they encountered.

Bernadette saw his somber expression and wondered at it. "You aren't having second thoughts?"

"About marrying you?" He smiled. "Of course

not. I was only thinking how wise we are not to pretend love for each other. Honesty is always best."

She mumbled her agreement, but she couldn't look him in the eye. It wouldn't do to tell him that she was head over heels in love with him and had been for as long as she could remember. He'd find it out one day. And hopefully, by then, he wouldn't mind. He might even learn to love her . . . a little.

She followed his intricate steps with ease, but it was a relief when other couples began to join them on the dance floor. She found herself breathless all too soon, and she hated the idea of people staring at her as she struggled to breathe.

He noticed when she began to pant softly. He also noticed that she never complained. She smiled at him and would have continued. But he stopped in mid-step and took her hand, placing it gently in the crook of his arm.

"And that's enough for now," he said with genuine affection. "We can sit on the sidelines and watch the others. Would you like some cold punch?"

"I would indeed!"

"You have a stubborn streak, Bernadette," he mused as they walked through the crowd of dancers. "I'm not sure it's a good thing. You push yourself too hard sometimes."

His voice was soft with concern and her heart lifted. He had to care for her a little, just a little. Her face brightened and became radiant. He glanced down at it and couldn't look away. Those eyes, those soft green eyes, had him all but hypnotized.

She was breathless all over again, but not from exertion this time. His eyes went from her face down to her white shoulders to the delicate cleavage between her pretty breasts.

It seemed that neither of them could forget those exquisite moments in the desert when he'd touched her in forbidden ways. It was in his face that he wanted that again.

Her fingers contracted on his sleeve, conveying her own inclinations.

He glanced at the patio doorway and back down at her. His face was hard, his black eyes glittering. He caught her gloved fingers in his.

"Shall we get a breath of air?" he asked evenly, surprised that his voice could sound so perfectly normal when he was churning inside.

"Yes, let's," she agreed at once.

He led her through the dancers again, smiling politely and not seeing a single face they passed.

The patio wasn't deserted. There were two couples dancing very close together. Eduardo gave them a wide berth and led Bernadette to the rose garden that was her pride and joy. There were high hedges and two large shade trees just beyond it, with a stone bench under one.

He seated her there. In the soft moonlight, her

face looked lovely. She was a little flushed, and her breathing was strained, but she was smiling.

"The scent of the roses isn't too overpowering for you?"

She shook her head. "I'm all right. I just got a little tired while we were dancing, that's all."

He looked around them. "It's lovely here. There's a rose bower at my grandmother's home in Granada, and a profusion of blooms swells there in the warmest month. There are orange and lemon trees."

"Did you take young women there?" she teased.

"Only one, my distant cousin Lupe," he replied lazily. "And her duenna," he added with a chuckle. "In Spain, no proper young lady goes anywhere with a gentleman unescorted."

"You told me that, once."

"But we are to be married," he reminded her softly. "And I hardly think this place is conducive to anything frightfully indiscreet. Although," he added, slowly removing his white gloves, "one never knows. Does one?"

His long, lean fingers traced the delicate line of her lips and then the curve of her soft chin, down her throat along the throbbing artery, to her collarbone. They rested there while his head moved closer to hers and she felt his breath on her mouth.

"Bernadette, you make me feel like a giant when I touch you."

"Why?"

"You melt against me. Your lips lift for mine. Your body inclines toward me. You tremble, and I can hear the very tenor of your breathing." His fingers trespassed slowly downward and he felt her jump under the intimate caress. "These are things no woman can pretend with a man. You want me very badly. It pleases me that you can't hide it."

She laughed nervously. "You are conceited."

"Not at all. I am . . . perceptive." His fingers moved again and his mouth caught the tiny cry that escaped her soft lips.

He kissed her with controlled ardor while his fingers trespassed inside her bodice and caught the hard thrust of her nipple between them. He caressed her. She leaned into him and moaned, clinging to him while his hand smoothed tenderly over the soft flesh.

When he felt her arch helplessly, he withdrew his invading hand and lifted his mouth from hers. He was having trouble breathing, too, and his body was telling him that this couldn't continue much longer.

He caressed her cheek gently as he searched her misty eyes and found tears glistening in them.

"It will be a good marriage," he said huskily.

"Yes."

He stood up abruptly with his back to her as he slipped his white gloves back on. His heart was ramming insistently against his ribcage and he felt swollen. Probably it was visible. He didn't dare go back into the ballroom until he had himself under better control. The thought of how easily he reacted to Bernadette amused him, and he laughed softly in the stillness of the garden.

"Why are you laughing?" she asked, rising to stand beside him.

He looked down at her. "I can't tell you until we're married."

"Oh, I see," she murmured, glancing down at him and then quickly away with a soft flush. "You think I'm blind."

He burst out laughing. "You wicked girl!"

She grinned at him mischievously. "And you said that I was responsive."

"And brazen," he teased. He linked his hand with hers. "Come. We'll stroll along through the roses until I can convince my starving body to contain its wicked appetite. I don't mind you seeing," he added gently, "but I don't care to advertise my state to the world at large."

She wondered at the comraderie they shared. She'd never dreamed there was a man who could take her through the emotions Eduardo had. They'd been adversaries, friends, conspirators, and soon they would be lovers.

Lovers.

The word ricocheted in her mind, trailing forbidden images. It would be sweet to lie in Eduardo's arms and let him do what he liked to her body. She knew already that he could give her pleasure in more than one way. But it was the consequence of intimacy that frightened her. It was the spectre of pregnancy. She remembered her sister's agony of long, painful, pitiful hours before she died. She remembered her father's harsh reminders of her mother's death at her own birth. The very thought of having a child made her terrified.

But when she looked at Eduardo, the thought of not having one was even sadder. He should have a son to replace the one he'd lost. He was the sort of man who would dote on a child, male or female. He wouldn't be like her father, blaming her and keeping her at arm's length for something that wasn't her fault. He was a fair man. He would be a good father. But she had to get past her fear to entertain even the idea of having a child with him. It wasn't going to be easy.

Chapter Seven

THE REST OF THE EVENING WAS DELIGHTFUL AND Bernadette moved through it like someone walking on air. Eduardo never left her side, not even when a pretty young Eastern socialite from one of the wealthiest families flirted with him.

Her father was obviously delighted at the number of monied and influential families who were enjoying his hospitality. He mingled, working so hard at trying to be one of them that his submissive attitude was almost comical. And it did seem to Bernadette as if the guests were only humoring him. They had nothing in common with him, something he didn't seem to realize. He might have money, but his background, though an honest and hardworking one, was still common. These people were of a social class that had never known deprivation or hardship, coming from families with noble or wealthy lineage. They talked about golf and about estates in England and Scotland, about foreign dignitaries and friends with whom they often visited.

Colston Barron might own some railroads but all he could talk about was the building of them. He knew the subject well, because he'd started as a poor Irish laborer on the eastern leg of the Union Pacific, working along with both Northern and Southern veterans of the War Between the States for three dollars an hour. He'd been in his late twenties when one of the railroads had gone into receivership. Colston had persuaded two foreigners to invest in the venture with him, and he'd plunged everything he could hock and beg and borrow into the bankrupt railroad. With a natural ability to talk his way out of any crisis and coax work out of the laziest of laborers, he'd parlayed that investment into a fortune for his backers, and then he'd bought them out. In his middle fifties now, he was as wealthy as many of his guests.

Of course, none of his guests had worked their way to fortune by the sweat of their brow. And when he spoke of his climb up from the ranks, he made his guests uncomfortable. It was a reminder that they were descendents of men like Colston, men whose determination and steely strength had built empires. Like Rockefeller and Carnegie, he was an empire-builder with the sort of focused determination most of them lacked. And, more, he was a mirror, reflecting their own weaknesses and inadequacies. He might have rough edges, but he was unique. They were only facsimiles of the men who had carved fortunes from raw iron and coal and steel. Consequently, they congregated among themselves and smiled politely when he joined their circles, and tried to find some common ground on which to build a conversation. But there was little. Bernadette's father seemed to realize it all at once, because he withdrew into himself and except for polite greetings as he passed his guests, he seemed very remote and unapproachable.

"He's not happy," Bernadette told Eduardo as they danced the last dance together, another graceful waltz that took her breath away.

"I know. He expects money to solve everything. It doesn't." He looked odd when he said that, and the glance he gave Bernadette was too complex to understand.

She didn't know that he was feeling more guilty by the minute for marrying her, when what he most needed was a loan and not a wife. He could give her affection, certainly, and a grand passion. But underneath it, there was nothing. Hers would be a barren existence, wealthy and honored, but without true happiness. He wished he could love her. It seemed like cheating to marry her only for a loan, even if he had been honest about his feelings.

She saw his expression and smiled up at him. "There you go feeling guilty again," she said with uncanny perception. "Will you stop worrying? I know what I'm doing, despite what you seem to think. I'm not asking for the stars, Eduardo. I'll have independence and a roof over my head and a husband handsome enough to make other women green with jealousy." She chuckled softly. "What more could I ask?"

"A lot, if you want the truth," he replied quietly. "It bothers me, this bargain of ours."

"It shouldn't. I'm willing to settle for what you've offered me. You can't let the ranch die. My father is your only hope of keeping it." She stared at his shirt front and decided that she might as well give him the option of backing out if he wanted to. "I think he might be willing to give you the loan without your having to marry me."

He caught his breath. The scowl he bent down on her head was genuinely angry. "I would refuse any such offer," he said curtly. "The bargain is that you marry me first. I have no intention of backing out of it. And neither," he added firmly, "are you going to. It's too late. You wear the family betrothal ring, and the bracelet. When I give my word, I keep it, Bernadette."

"Yes, I know, but you were forced into this."

"I was not. I could have gone to my grandmother. I could still go."

"And sacrifice your pride," she said irritably. "Go begging. I'd rather you starved."

Her vehemence on his behalf amused him. His arm pulled her perceptibly closer. "Would you? And would you starve with me, my intended bride?"

"Of course," she said with simple honesty. "That's what marriage is supposed to be about."

His face looked briefly drawn and solemn. "Consuela would have gone to her parents at once, rather than face such a comedown."

She pinched his arm. "I'm not Conseula, nor am I likely to be," she said. "Would you mind not comparing us? It's uncomfortable."

"Not half as uncomfortable as I would be should you become like her."

She was remembering what he'd told her about the other woman in their moments of intimacy and she flushed uncomfortably.

He saw her expression and his was puzzled. "I should not have said such a thing to you. It was indecent. But I thought you should know the truth. It was hardly a love match, before or after. And no, I didn't kill her."

"I never thought you did. You need not have told me a second time."

"Why do you always defend me?" he asked, his face hard and still. "You don't really know me, Bernadette. There are dark places in my soul which are very seldom brought into the light. You may find it difficult to live with me."

"I find it difficult to live with my father," she reminded him. "You'll be a picnic compared to my past life, however ungrateful that sounds." She put her handkerchief to her mouth and coughed. The exercise of dancing was producing still more breathlessness and she was afraid she might have an attack.

"We'll stop now," he said gently, leading her off the dance floor. "You've done remarkably well tonight, considering the smell of all these heavy perfumes." He frowned. "Are you going to be all right?"

"Certainly." She coughed again. "I'll have Maria bring me some coffee and I'll sit quietly while the guests prepare to leave. Those who aren't staying with us," she qualified.

"I'll see Maria. You sit here." He eased her into a chair and walked off in the general direction of the kitchen.

The guests left rather quickly, all aglow with the latest news to carry back to their respective homes. Bernadette marrying a Spanish nobleman, and how exciting to have such a grand event held so near their homes!

Bernadette took the congratulations in her stride, but she noticed that her father was positively morose.

After the room had cleared of guests, Colston joined Bernadette and Eduardo in the parlor.

"Did you enjoy yourself, Father?"

He grimaced. "Sure and what a bunch of peacocks preening," he muttered with a self-conscious glance at them. "I've never been so uncomfortable in me life. All that talk of golf and race horses and tennis and fancy hotels! And such fine clothes and parlor manners, from men whose hands were as lily white as a rich woman's!"

"Those people didn't make their fortunes, they inherited them," Bernadette pointed out.

"So I see." He turned to her. "At least it wasn't all for naught," he added, glancing at Eduardo with a smile. "I get a fine son-in-law for my pains, and someone to inherit this place when I'm gone."

"What about Albert?" Bernadette asked, surprised.

"Do you think he'd ever come back here to live?" he scoffed. "His father-in-law has given him a ship and he's become a fisherman. Says he never loved anything so much. He'd sell this place and never grieve. Eduardo wouldn't," he added, his gaze going to the younger man standing beside Bernadette. "He loves the land. He'd make it pay, just as I have."

"I might not succeed," Eduardo told him. "But it wouldn't be for lack of trying." He looked down at Bernadette's wan face. "This child needs her bed, and I have to return home. It was a fine party," he told Colston.

"Indeed, Father, and it was kind of you to turn your ball into our engagement party," Bernadette added.

Colston shrugged. "I feel a fool. I've never swallowed so much pride in me life. I'm for bed and a hot toddy. Is Maria still in the kitchen?"

"Yes," Eduardo said, indicating the cup of black coffee Bernadette was sipping, which Maria had made for her.

Colston shifted restlessly. "You'll need to watch her around flowers," he told Eduardo with surprising concern. "She loves them and spends too much time puttering about them, mucking in the earth. She'll pay for it with several days in bed."

"I'll take care of her."

"I'll take care of myself," Bernadette told her fiancé. "I don't want to spend my life fighting my lungs. I won't be any trouble at all."

Colston looked guilty. He murmured a polite good night and left the two of them alone.

Eduardo looked down at her with some concern. "I'll have Maria listen out for you tonight, just in case. I'll see you tomorrow."

She smiled at him. "Yes."

He bent swiftly and brushed a soft kiss across her forehead. "Sleep well, Bernadette."

"You, too."

He put a lean hand on her shoulder and squeezed it gently before he rose and followed her father to the kitchen. He was going to make sure before he left that Maria would take care of his intended. Despite Colston's reassurances, he wasn't convinced that the man had his daughter's best interests at heart.

* * *

Eduardo's behavior at the ball had lightened Bernadette's step and given her hope for their future. But only two days later, her world shattered. Eduardo came with a buggy to get her and take her to meet guests who had arrived far earlier than expected—just the day before.

"My grandmother is here," he told Bernadette and her father. He was stiff and very formal, as if the atmosphere at Rancho Escondido had already changed drastically. "She would like to meet my intended bride. I have promised to fetch Bernadette."

"Well, of course she wants to meet her," Colston said. "Get your bonnet, girl, and go with Eduardo."

Bernadette needed no prompting. She was eager to meet the grandmother of whom Eduardo had so often spoken. Not that she wasn't a little intimidated by the prospect, especially since Eduardo already seemed different.

Eduardo's ranch was far from the familiar dirt road, back in a box canyon where mesquite and willow trees provided shade for a large adobe structure with hanging baskets of flowers. It was elegant and grand, with imported wood for the doors and shutters, and a porch that Bernadette had always loved, the sort of house she wished her father had built, instead of the Victorian horror he liked so much.

Eduardo helped her out at the front steps and

gave the horse-drawn buggy to a servant to put away. He escorted Bernadette onto the porch and hesitated just before they entered.

"She is Spanish to her very toes," he told her in a brittle tone. "She may be a trial to you at first. Be patient."

"Of course."

She went inside with him, down the grand hall with its elegant mahogany staircase, into a large room with heavy rosewood furniture and silk draperies. There was a Persian rug on the spotless wood floor that was obviously imported and very expensive. And there, on the rose-pink silk couch was a tiny white-haired woman in a black silk dress, looking at Bernadette as if she'd like to take a fire poker to her.

"This is my grandmother, the Condessa Dolores Maria Cortes. Abuela, my intended, Bernadette Barron."

Bernadette started to extend a hand, but that stiff little woman never moved an inch. She inclined her head. She said nothing. Her eyes spoke for her.

Eduardo's hand touched Bernadette's lightly where it fell at her side. "My grandmother has only arrived from Spain and she is very tired," he said firmly. "Besides," he added shrewdly, "her English is not very good."

The old lady gave him a glare that would have felled a lesser man. She sat erect. "My English is perfect," she said in a voice that was only slightly accented. "I do not like the language, but I can use it!"

"As we see," Eduardo replied. He stared at his grandmother until she shifted restlessly.

"You are to marry my grandson, Señorita Barron," the old woman said tightly. "You are not Spanish."

"My ancestry is Irish," the younger woman agreed.

"My son broke with tradition and married an American girl," the condessa said with blatant disapproval. "A butterfly with no morals and no sense of family or tradition. And you see the result!" She waved around her at the grand, but obviously worn, furniture and draperies. "She was a profligate. She spent my son's money and drove him to despair. . . . She broke his heart."

Bernadette felt immediately on the defensive. She clasped her hands together tightly at her waist and lifted her chin. "I am neither immoral nor heartless," she informed the old woman. "I intend to be a good wife."

One white eyebrow lifted. "Do you?" she asked mockingly.

Eduardo started to speak when a door opened and a beautiful young woman in a yellow silk dress swept into the room. She had startling black hair and eyes, in a face like an angel's.

"Eduardo! How lovely to see you again!"

She came forward in a cloud of heavy perfume, smiling—and ignoring the other two women present. The young woman rose onto tiptoe and kissed Eduardo full on the mouth, shocking Bernadette.

"Lupe!" the condessa exclaimed, outraged.

"Oh, do not be so stuffy, Tía Dolores!" Lupe chided. She clasped Eduardo's arm tightly against her breasts. "I have not seen him for two years."

"Lupe de Rias, this is my betrothed, Bernadette Barron," Eduardo introduced the newcomer to Bernadette, his manner even stiffer and more formal than it had been.

"How nice to meet you, señorita," Lupe said, but her eyes weren't smiling. She went forward to offer a languid hand to Bernadette, smothering her in thick perfume and bringing on a violent coughing spasm.

Eduardo yelled for his servant and demanded coffee be brought quickly. He moved Bernadette away from the others and into a deep chair, kneeling beside her and clasping her hands tightly in his own.

"Breathe gently, Bernadette," he said calmly "Gently. It's all right."

"What is wrong with her?" the condessa demanded imperiously.

"She is an asthmatic," Eduardo said through his teeth, because he hadn't mentioned this affliction to his grandmother.

"Asthmatic!" The old woman got to her feet and walked to Eduardo's side. "An invalid? What are you thinking? She cannot give you children!"

Eduardo looked scandalized. "You must surely be tired from your long journey. Why do you not let Lupe take you upstairs now? You need your rest."

The condessa glared at him. "I am not tired. Look at her! She cannot even breathe! What sort of mistress will she make for the Rancho Escondido?"

"Will you please go to your room?" Eduardo asked, and this time there was a clear threat underneath the polite tone.

Unintimidated, the old woman folded her hands and looked down her nose at him. "Very well. I shall rest for an hour. But then you and I must talk."

"Shall I stay, Eduardo?" Lupe asked. "Perhaps I could do something."

"Lupe, it is your perfume that has brought on the problem," Eduardo said gently. "I know it was not intentional, but it will only make this worse if you do not leave right away."

Lupe wasn't offended at all. She smiled. "Certainly. I would not want to worsen Bernadette's condition. Poor little thing," she added, all condolences. "What a shame, too, that she is so frail. Still, you will take care of her, yes? And the servants will help. Perhaps a good nurse as well, to watch over her when your duties demand your time?"

"Yes, yes, that might be a good idea, Lupe. Now, if you please?"

Lupe looked triumphant. "I shall help you find the right nurse for her. It will be my pleasure! But do you think we should go ahead with the wedding plans now? It might be prudent to wait a few months—"

"Now!"

Lupe shifted. "As you wish, of course. I'll leave you, then."

She went out, closing the door behind her.

Bernadette had heard the conversation but taken no part in it. She was occupied just trying to keep her breath. So that was Eduardo's grandmother and cousin. The scorpion and the pit viper. She wished she had the breath to laugh. No wonder he'd been landed with a bride like Consuela. Those two conspirators had probably put their heads together and made him the worst match in the history of his family. He'd said that his grandmother favored his cousin Luis to inherit her wealth. Probably she'd gone out of her way to make Eduardo's life difficult so that Luis would be the obvious choice and there would be no gossip about her decision.

She wondered why the old woman had come all this way, and why Lupe had been chosen to make the wedding arrangements. Well, Eduardo's cousin and grandmother were in for a surprise. Bernadette wasn't going to be led around by the nose, and she wasn't going to permit those two to destroy his life. They'd done all the damage they were going to be permitted to do. She looked at him through wet eyes and thought how drawn and worn he already looked.

She lay her hand gently against his cheek. He started, as if the gesture shocked him.

"Poor man," she said hoarsely.

He scowled. His hand pressed hers closer. "Why do you say that?"

"Never mind." She managed a smile. "Does Lupe bathe in perfume, do you think?"

He smiled for the first time in several minutes. "I think she must. Odd, I don't remember her wearing so much in the past. But as she said, it has been two years."

"She's beautiful."

"Indeed."

Bernadette didn't say anything. The servant came in with the coffee and she sat and sipped it until her lungs felt less constrained and she could breathe almost normally again.

"I don't suppose you would like to stay for dinner?" he asked.

She studied his face. "I don't think so," she replied gently, because now that Lupe knew how that heavy perfume affected her, she'd put on even more of it for the evening meal. Knowing the enemy was half the battle. Bernadette had to search out some armor before she'd be ready to deal with this bunch.

"It's just as well. They're tired," he added. "Come. I'll drive you home."

They started back toward the Barron ranch, but Eduardo pulled off beside a small stream under some trees and sat quietly for a minute, with the reins wrapped around the brake.

"Are you truly all right?" he asked her.

She smiled. "I'm fine." She took a long breath. "See?" She searched his eyes. "And I won't need a nurse," she added firmly.

"I have noticed that your health improves when you and I are alone," he replied, studying her. "Your father upsets you. So do my grandmother and Lupe. But none of them will live with us."

She wondered if she should tell him her suspicions, that the women would plot to prevent the marriage. She decided not to. There was time for that later. Besides, Eduardo cared for her. He wasn't going to let himself be influenced by his family, no matter how much he cared for them. That he'd followed his grandmother's wishes and married Consuela was something she refused to think about.

"I'll have Lupe start on the arrangements tomorrow. She'll need a list of guests whom you and your father wish to invite. The ceremony will be held in San Antonio," he added firmly, "at the

Cathedral of San Fernando. There is no place here that will hold the number of guests we should anticipate. It will be a social occasion, a very grand one. You must have a gown that does justice to you, Bernadette. Lupe will get you one from Madrid." His eyes slid over her slender body with delight. "Your fairness will be truly lovely in white lace," he added.

"You don't want to back out, while there's still time?" she asked, worried.

He thought of all the gossip about their night on the plateau, drew her protectively close, and sighed. "No, I don't want to back out." He bent his head and kissed her gently. His head lifted, but only a fraction. He caught her arms and guided them up around his shoulders before he bent again. This time the kiss was more intimate, more insistent. He nipped her lower lip and moved at once inside it, coaxing her mouth open to permit the slow, steady penetration of his tongue.

She moaned and held him closer. She felt his mouth smile against hers, felt the increase of his pulse. Her own raced and she was breathless, but not because of her lungs.

His hands slid up her ribcage to caress her breasts with lazy delight.

She looked up into his eyes through a dazed mist as he caressed her.

"No more protests, Bernadette?" he teased softly.

She smiled lazily. "I like it," she whispered. "Should I pretend that I don't until we're married?"

"That would be a waste of time," he pointed out with a smile of his own. He looked down at the softness in his hands ruefully. "What I wouldn't give to taste them. But considering the turn of my luck lately, a carriage full of gossips would drive by the second I put my mouth on you."

She chuckled. "You are wonderfully wicked."

"Oh, yes." He kissed her once more, savoring her mouth, and moved away with obvious reluctance. "I must take you home. Before I get any more wicked ideas."

"How long are your grandmother and Lupe going to stay?" she asked, because it was as well to find out now.

"For the summer," he said, confirming her worst fears. He glanced at her with a smile. "They won't intrude when we're married. We'll have an entire wing of our own, far away from them."

"Well, that's all right, then."

He picked up the reins and guided the horse back onto the narrow dirt road. "I'm truly sorry that things went so badly this afternoon with my grandmother," he told her. "She's old and she has fixed ideas about marriage. You'll get used to her."

"I'm sure I will," she lied.

He glanced at her and smiled. "She's not so bad,

Bernadette. She had a hard life with my grandfather. He kept a mistress the whole of their married life. When my father was born, my grandfather was off traveling with the woman."

"Was your father an only child?"

He nodded. "His death was a vicious blow to her, especially the way it occurred: My mother's scandalous behavior, my father's decline, then his sudden demise."

"Yes," she said sadly. "It must have been terrible for your grandmother . . . and for you."

"It was. My mother never wept, never grieved, never offered me or anyone else comfort. She was far too preoccupied with her lover of the moment." His face hardened. "I was eight years old."

She grimaced. "I could never leave my child alone under those . . . or any other circumstances," she said absently, thinking aloud.

"I know that. But she could, and did. She went to New York." He stared ahead with cold eyes. "I haven't seen her or heard from her in all those years. She closed the door between us and never looked back. My grandmother classes all American women with her and hates the idea of my marrying you for that reason."

"I understand," she said, and did. "I'll try to get along with your family, Eduardo."

"They have faults," he said. "But Abuela matters to me, just as your father and brother matter in many ways to you." He scowled. "Will you let your brother know about our marriage?"

"Of course. I'll write to him. Albert and I are so far apart in age that we've never been really close. But he'll remember you," she assured him. "And I think he'll be happy for me. I am for him. He and my father never got along, especially after my sister was forced to marry against her will."

He frowned. "Tell me truly, you aren't allowing your father to make you do something you don't want to? Our marriage has your consent as well as his?"

"You know it does," she said firmly. "My father isn't really a bad man. Perhaps he will learn one day that we are not the masters of our own destiny. There's a divinity that shapes events and people."

"You know that, at your age, and he hasn't learned it."

She chuckled. "My father is a conundrum." She glanced at him mischieviously. "Like your grandmother."

He shook his head. "What a tangle we have to work our way through to marry. But we will," he added, smiling at her. "And we're going to build our ranch into an empire. You will see."

"I can't wait," she said enthusiastically. She averted her eyes so that he wouldn't see the love shining out of them.

Chapter Eight

BERNADETTE WAS VERY UNEASY ABOUT HAVING Eduardo's grandmother and Lupe in residence while the marriage arrangements were made. She knew in her heart that the two women were going to make things as difficult as possible for her. She wasn't afraid of them, or intimidated by them, but she was wary. And she didn't want to alienate Eduardo's family.

On the other hand, remembering the old woman's cold attitude toward her, she knew that she wasn't going to be able to tolerate insults without a challenge. Regardless of the condessa's place in Eduardo's life, Bernadette wasn't going to let the woman make her life hell. She'd had quite enough of being treated like a contagious disease by her own father.

A week later, her father came home from Eduardo's house with a strange look on his face. He called Bernadette into his study and offered her a seat at his desk. He looked truly concerned.

"I want to know," he began hesitantly, "if you still want to go through with the marriage."

She lifted both eyebrows. "Why?"

"Because I've just met that little black scorpion from Spain," he said through his teeth. His face reddened with temper. "And I think you're going to have a hell of a time living with her, even for the summer."

Bernadette stared at him with faint amusement. "Why, Father," she said, "did you get it in the neck, too?"

He cleared his throat, locked his hands behind his back, and paced. "That venomous woman!" he muttered. "Looking down her nose at me as if I were one of her damned peons, and telling her grandson—in front of me, mind you!—that I hardly looked the part of a wealthy gentleman!"

"That's nothing to what she said about me," she replied with a rueful smile. "She didn't like me at all. And when her niece came in wearing a gallon of heavy perfume, I had an attack." She grimaced. "Lupe told Eduardo that he'd have to hire a nurse for me."

"The damned insolence!"

She glanced at him. "Well, you used to say the same thing."

He looked uncomfortable. "Perhaps I've been a bit . . . unfair in the past," he conceded. "But whatever my own feelings, those women have no right to sit in judgment of us, or to make rude remarks about you. Or about me!"

Bernadette felt, for the first time, an affectionate kinship with him. How different her father had been since she and Eduardo had become engaged. At last, she said, "She doesn't approve of me, and she doesn't like the idea of my marrying Eduardo, regardless of how much money you're willing to loan him," she said on a heavy breath. She glanced down at her small hands folded neatly in her lap. "I must admit, I found her very heavy going. And Lupe—"

"She wants Eduardo," he interrupted with a hard look. "Did you know?"

"It's hard to miss. She pretends to be friendly, but it's all a ruse, and I'm not sure that Eduardo knows it. They're the only family he has left that he's willing to claim, and I don't want to have words with him about her. But if she's allowed to order my wedding gown, I expect I'll go to the altar in one that's two sizes off and of a design to make me look ridiculous."

"She won't have any say about the gown."

"But—"

He held up a hand. "I'll say what's to be done. You'll go to New York to shop for it. I'll have my secretary at my office in San Antonio book passage for you in our private train car. Maria can go with you. I'll have one of the vaqueros' wives take over her duties in the kitchen. There's only me to cook for anyway, with all the visitors finally gone."

Bernadette was uncomfortable at the thought of traveling so far alone. "I don't want to go," she said miserably.

"It's that or let Lupe pick out the dress herself."

She got up. "That's no choice at all," she said heavily. "Very well, I'll go."

"There's a specialist there, a doctor who has had some great successes dealing with asthmatics," he added surprisingly. "You can see him as well."

She was astounded. He hadn't taken any notice of her health for years, except to complain about it. "Do you mean it?"

He averted his eyes as if his comment embarrassed him. "'Course I do. Go on, then, start packing. You'll leave tomorrow. I'll telegraph now to get the arrangements underway."

"But what about Eduardo?" she asked worriedly. She had visions of the women talking him out of marrying her while she was gone.

"He'll still be here when you come back. You can stay at the Waldorf-Astoria. I'll telegraph straight to them to get a reservation for you."

"You're being very kind, Father."

"You're the only daughter I have left," he replied gruffly. "Can't see you married in rags, can I? Not in the biggest cathedral in San Antonio."

"Oh, I see."

He glared at her. "No, you don't. I want you to do

me proud, sure I do, but I'm not having you made a laughingstock by that haughty Spanish miss!"

She wasn't sure what to say. It was still like talking to a stranger. "I won't be."

"This whole affair is my fault." He stared down at his boots. "I thought getting myself into high social circles would make me acceptable to the better families. I never realized until the ball how wrong I was about that." He lifted pale eyes to her. "I haven't a thing in common with them. We're as different as night and day. I had to earn what I have. They inherited it, most of them. The Culhanes and I get along, of course, because the old man made his fortune the way I made mine. But, then, they're not exactly overwhelmed with invitations from back East, either."

"I think it was as hard for your guests that night," she said. "It isn't that they don't think you're good enough to be invited to social events, Father, it's that you don't share the same interests. They know nothing about cattle and you know nothing about golf." She smiled. "Perhaps you might get some clubs and learn to play. Surely someone in San Antonio has a course of some sort to play. Isn't there a man named Cumming Macdonough who brought the game over from Scotland a few years ago and built a golf course there with his sons?"

"Yes, by golly, there is! And he knows the game better than anybody hereabouts. Lass, you're a constant wonder to me! I'll go looking for him this very weekend!"

She grinned. "That's the way to get into exalted circles—learn the games they play and beat them at it."

He chuckled. "So I'm discovering." He searched her eyes, so like her mother's. "Bernadette, I've never given you much reason to think that I care what happens to you. But I do care. There's time to back out of this marriage. I won't say a word, and I'll still give Eduardo his loan."

"I made him the same offer. He refused. He says that he gave his word and he won't go back on it."

"But you don't mind marrying him, then?"

She smiled sadly. "I love him with all my heart," she confessed. "I have for years. Even if he can't return my feelings, he's fond of me. Maybe one day . . ." She hesitated. "Maybe there can be a child. At least one child, to inherit."

He scowled. He didn't say a word, but he was seeing his beautiful Eloise screaming in pain.

"I must go and plan what to take with me," she said hurriedly, because she saw the look and misunderstood it entirely. "Thank you for letting me get my own gown, Father. I'm very grateful."

"It's little enough to do, girl. God knows, I've done almost nothing for you." He turned back to the window. "Nothing cheap, mind. Get a gown to turn Lupe pea green with envy."

"Yes, sir, I shall!" She opened the door and

paused. "If Eduardo comes, you'll explain to him? I mean, without making Lupe sound like a devil?"

He chuckled. "I'll do me best," he murmured. "She is a devil, though."

"I know it. But he mustn't. His family is very important to him. I wouldn't want to do anything to upset him."

"From what I've seen of them, you may not be able to prevent it." He glanced at her. "You're my daughter, mind, and you have my temper. I can't see you letting the old woman walk all over you."

"Nor can I. Perhaps she'll go home right after the wedding," she said hopefully.

"Lass, I wouldn't hold my breath waiting for that to happen."

She sighed. "I know what you mean."

The train trip took four days each way. Allowing for the time in transit and the visit to the dressmaker and the physician who specialized in treatment of lung diseases it was a two-week sojourn. What a wonderful luxury to ride in her father's private railroad car, which was attached to a train bound for St. Louis, Missouri, and then transferred to a car headed east. It was fascinating to watch the porters her father employed working with such brisk efficiency to transform the car to serve all her needs. It was, Bernadette fancied, the way royalty would travel.

New York City amazed . . . intimidated . . .

thrilled the two women from southwest Texas. Maria was delighted with the wedding dress Bernadette chose. It was exquisitely embroidered with white roses, and covered with Belgian lace. There was a veil that fell to her hips in front and ran down to the scalloped edges of the satin train in back. The high neck was embroidered and covered with delicate lace, as were the mutton sleeves and flaring skirt. It was horribly expensive. But as her father had said, Bernadette reminded herself, she was only marrying once. And this was a gown to grace a princess.

It was fitted, altered, packed, and sent to the railway station when Bernadette and Maria were ready to leave.

Meanwhile, Bernadette had seen Dr. Harold Metter, a young physician with some new ideas about the treatment of asthma that were attracting much attention in the medical community. He prescribed sedatives and had an order made up for Bernadette, along with a prescription to take home with her. The drug was an opiate, so it was imperative that she use it only when everything else failed, he instructed. He also prescribed moderate exercise and fresh air and a light diet.

Bernadette felt more confident about herself than she ever had before. She also worked up enough courage to ask the physician about the possibility of having a child. He said there was no reason she shouldn't, even when told about her family medical history. He examined her and pronounced her quite fit enough to carry a child without endangering her life. Here, again, he had revolutionary theories, and one of them was that she must keep active right up until the birth of a child. If she would contact him by mail when she knew herself to be pregnant, he would prescribe a course of exercises to make the birth easier, as well as refer her to a prominent obstetrician in San Antonio.

Bernadette went back to Valladolid County feeling as if she were floating the whole way. She had her exquisite wedding gown and the hope of a normal life, babies, and a happy marriage. All she had to do was get around the old condessa and the young Lupe, and win Eduardo's heart. Buoyed by optimism, she felt she could accomplish anything. It was just a matter of planning, she told herself. And she was ready to start a campaign.

The dress was admired by her father and pronounced perfect. He was also surprised by the physician's recommendations, and delighted by the prognosis. He seemed genuinely touched by the positive turns in her life.

Eduardo rode over to see her the day following her return. He looked perfectly normal until he spoke to her. He was remote, formal, so correct that he seemed a stranger.

They sat together in the living room, sipping the

coffee that Maria had brought from the kitchen, and neither spoke for several minutes.

"You found a gown, I understand?" he asked finally, his stiffness tinged with anger.

"Well, yes." She wondered at his attitude. "Didn't Father explain to you that I wanted to choose my own gown?"

"Certainly he explained. However, my cousin Lupe was deeply offended by this shopping trip. She helped to purchase the gown for the king's niece, and I assure you, she found a gown befitting royalty."

She folded her hands on the lap of her pale-blue dress and stared at him without backing down an inch. "I daresay she was eager to please the king," she said with emphasis.

His eyebrows lifted. "Are you insinuating that she wouldn't be eager to please me?"

"I don't doubt it. But I wanted to choose my own gown."

He stared at her unblinking for several long seconds before he spoke again, with less belligerence. "She wept, you know," he murmured. "My grandmother was very upset as well. She said that your father most likely had a low opinion of Spanish people and distrusted our taste."

"Bosh," she said irritably.

"Bosh?"

She waved a hand. "I mean, he thought no such thing. It was my idea to go to New York," she lied.

"The dress was only a subterfuge I used to get my father to agree to the trip. I saw a specialist while I was there, Eduardo." Her enthusiasm shone out of her green eyes like beacons. She leaned forward. "He gave me sedatives to take when I have an attack, and he told me how to build up my lungs so that the attacks lessen!" She wanted to tell him that she could even have a child without fear, but she was suddenly tongue-tied on the subject—especially as he wasn't acting like the Eduardo she'd known for so many years.

"This is good news," he said eventually. "But should you take sedatives when you can barely breathe?"

"He's a very good doctor," she replied. "One of the president's relations is attended by him. He's had many successes with his treatment."

"Then I agree that the trip wasn't wasted." He put down his coffee cup. He looked tired, and not too happy.

"Aren't things going well at the ranch?" she asked hesitantly.

His black eyes lifted to hers, then narrowed. "My grandmother is distressed that I decided to take a wife before I discussed it with her." He leaned back. "She brought Lupe on the trip with her with the idea that we would become engaged."

A cold chill went down Bernadette's spine. She felt her body go numb from the impact of the words.

"Lupe is Spanish," he continued. "She has poise and breeding and great wealth. And my grandmother believed that I would see now the error of my ways in rejecting Lupe and then marrying Consuela."

Bernadette's temper, never mild, exploded. She got to her feet in one swift movement and turned to march to the door.

"Where are you going?" Eduardo demanded, rising.

She opened the door and turned her furious eyes toward him. "Obviously your grandmother has more influence over you than I have. Marry Lupe, then. Perhaps she'll turn out to be as wonderful a wife as Consuela. Your grandmother also chose her for you, I believe?"

She stomped down the hall, barely aware of hard footsteps behind her. When she was even with the pantry, a lean hand grasped her arm firmly and she was shoved gently into the pantry and Eduardo closed the door behind them.

"You uncivilized little tigress," Eduardo muttered angrily, pressing her back against the shelves full of canned fruit and vegetables. The room was small and dimly lit, stifling with the heat. But neither of them noticed.

"Let me go!" she grumbled, struggling. "Lupe is everything you want, you said so, why don't you rush home and put a ring on her finger? Here, I'll give it back!"

She tugged at the ring on her engagement finger, but as she lifted her hands to struggle with the tightly fitted piece of jewelry, Eduardo's head bent. He found her soft mouth and opened it under the furious pressure of his lips.

She hit at him, but he caught her hands and drew them behind her, holding her helpless while his mouth fed on hers. Her knees felt as if they might collapse as the hard, ardent kiss went on and on. His strong hands went to her back and captured her, enveloping her against the power of his body.

"Oh, you rogue!" she ground out against his mouth.

He only kissed her harder. His hips pressed into hers, imprisoning her against the hard wood of the shelves. He moved even closer, one long leg going between hers so that she was in a new and startling intimacy with him. When his hips shifted, his arousal became quite noticeable.

She stiffened, despite the languor his kisses had invoked in her.

He felt her withdrawal and lifted his head. He was breathing as roughly as she was, and his eyes were glittering with desire as they searched hers.

"Now send me to Lupe," he whispered, so close that his breath made tiny chills against her moist lips.

She could barely get words past her tongue. Her body felt swollen and trembly. She could feel how aroused he was, and she was embarrassed. "Please," she whispered. "You must stop. . . ."

"Must I?" He looked into her eyes and deliberately moved even closer, so that she felt him in a way he'd never permitted her to until now. "Do you feel it, Bernadette?" he taunted huskily. "Do you know what it wants?"

"Eduardo!" she gasped.

"All that magnificent passion, wasted in anger, when it could be so profitably employed in a quite different fashion," he whispered, bending again. "Open your mouth, Bernadette. Put your hands against what you feel and touch me."

"You . . . blackguard!" She struggled, but it only made matters worse. He groaned and his ardor was suddenly insistent.

She moaned piteously against the penetration of his tongue. Her body clenched at the sensations the suggestive kiss raised in her virginal body. It was like that night in the desert, when he'd held her and caressed her so hungrily. But now her body found his familiar, and she welcomed the caresses that would once have torn her from his arms in shame.

She trembled as his hands searched for buttons at her throat and began to unfasten them. The room was hot, so hot. She could barely breathe for the heat. And then his mouth found her throat and worked its way down the path of the buttons until he moved it right inside her dress, into her bodice, against her bare breast.

She shivered and moaned loudly. Her fingers caught in his thick hair and she pulled at his head, coaxing it, her body moving, shifting, to bring him where it wanted his mouth.

"Please," she choked out. "Please, here . . . here . . . just a little farther . . . !"

Her hands guided him blindly until his mouth was on the hard, swollen nipple.

"Here?" he whispered huskily. "Here, Bernadette?" He began to suckle her, tasting her soft skin, and she arched up to him hungrily.

"Yes," she sobbed. "Yes, yes, yes!"

His mouth was the center of the universe. It was wicked, what they were doing, but she wanted it. Oh, how she wanted it! She wanted her bodice down around her waist, and his mouth all over her breasts. She wanted his eyes, his hands, his mouth on every inch of her body. . . .

He groaned at the fever they were kindling. He moved her into the light from the high window and his hands efficiently moved the blouse and the straps of her cotton slip and chemise aside. She hadn't bothered with her usual corset because of the awful heat, and now that he knew it, he was glad. He pulled the straps down to her waist and caught his breath at the sight of those firm, pretty, red-tipped breasts.

"Dear God, Bernadette," he whispered. He

touched them reverently, caressing them with tenderness and awe.

She shivered, her hands clutching at his sleeves as the magic of his touch worked on her body and made her ache in her most feminine places.

She arched her back, her eyes half-closed, drowning in the delicious sensation of being seen intimately by him. "Please . . . Eduardo," she whispered, pulling at his head.

He looked into her wide eyes. "What do you want, amada?" he whispered softly. "My mouth on your breasts, like this, with no clothing to dull the sensation?"

"Yes," she said brokenly. "Oh, yes!"

"It is what I want as well, the taste of you, like warm petals on my tongue." He bent and slowly opened his mouth against the silky skin, feeling her immediate response, hearing her soft cries, enjoying the taste and scent of her.

He was slow and thorough. She felt as if she'd died and gone right to heaven in his arms as he teased and touched and tasted and explored her with tenderness.

"Such exquisite skin," he murmured against her body. "Soft and warm and scented like roses. I want all of you, Bernadette. I want to feel your body soft and naked under mine in my bed. I want to possess you absolutely."

She should have been shocked by the passionate words. But she was only aroused more. Her arms slid around his neck and she met his ravishing mouth with all the clumsy ardor she could manage, loving the taste of him, the feel of him.

The sudden sound of loud footsteps and even louder voices out in the hall made them fly apart. Eduardo seemed dazed, which in fact he was. His black eyes studied Bernadette's bare breasts as if they were incapable of anything else. He touched her again, with quiet wonder, even as the footsteps became louder.

She started to speak, but he put his finger over her lips and they both held their breath until the footsteps, which had paused briefly at the pantry, suddenly went past and on down the hall toward the living room.

"Too close," he murmured softly. He searched her eyes with a rueful smile. "So much for restraint." He looked down at her breasts and shook his head as he began to pull the chemise and the slip back up to cover her. "How beautiful you are, Bernadette. The sight of you makes a madman of me."

She was bereft of words. She watched him dressing her with a sense of unreality. It wasn't until the buttons were once more fastened that her heart began to beat normally. She was breathless, but not dangerously so. She looked up at him helplessly, with longing and adoration.

He met that soft glance squarely and smiled

gently. "It delights me that you have no experience at coyness," he said. "When I touch you, you deny me nothing. It bodes well for the future."

"Are we going to have one?"

He nodded. "Because I can't give you up, regardless of my grandmother's feelings." He added, "I owe her a great deal, you understand. But marrying Lupe to repay her is more gratitude than I am capable of giving her." He traced around Bernadette's soft, swollen lips. "You make my blood race like wildfire through my body. I ache for you, night and day. The wedding must be soon, for the sake of your chastity and my own honor. This," he indicated their surroundings, "was a near thing."

She was puzzled. "A near thing? But it would be impossible for anything indiscreet to happen here." She laughed nervously. "There's not even a . . . a bed!"

"Oh, Bernadette." He chuckled. "How innocent you are."

"But there isn't any place . . . Eduardo!"

While she was telling him why they couldn't, he picked her up by the waist and pinned her to the wall with his hips.

He kissed her gently and let her down again, smiling at her red-faced realization.

"It is possible to make love while standing," he whispered, laughing at her shocked gasp. "And in many other unlikely places and positions. Once we're married, I'll show you all of them."

She tried to find words, and couldn't get them past her surprise. He smoothed her hair and her dress, opened the door, peered carefully down the hall, and tugged her out with him.

They walked together quite circumspectly to the front porch. "Don't come out with me," he said. "It's much too hot out there." He lifted her hand to his mouth and kissed her fingers softly. "I am a most lucky man," he said with solemn fervor. "And I'll do my best to make you feel that you're the luckiest woman alive."

Her heart skipped a beat. "You aren't angry anymore, about the dress?"

"After this?" He laughed. "No, Bernadette. I'm not angry about the dress. I'll come back in a day or two to fetch you. We still have to make final the guest list, invitations, and a few other arrangements."

"I thought Lupe was going to do it all," she said, trying not to sound bitter or jealous.

"Not now. It's your wedding. I think you should decide some of these things." He looked at her hungrily. "I only want it to be quick."

She smiled. "So do I!"

He shook his head slowly, marveling at the passion they kindled in each other. It was a magnificent thing that a man and a woman should pleasure each other so much in that relatively innocent way. The thought of Bernadette in his bed made his head swim, made his body clench hard with desire. She was going to be sweet heaven to make love to. He could scarcely wait to make her his wife.

She saw that need in him and her face became radiant. "I'll try not to disappoint you, even though I'm not Spanish."

He chuckled. "That doesn't matter to me."

"It does to your grandmother."

His smile faded. "Cross bridges when you come to them," he counseled. "There's no need to borrow trouble."

"That's the last thing I want to do." She took a step forward. "I'll try to get along with your grandmother. I promise I will."

"I know that." He smiled at her. "Adiós."

"Adiós."

His eyes narrowed. "You might learn a little of our language," he said thoughtfully. "That would impress her."

She already read and spoke it like a native, but she wasn't giving away that secret just yet. It still might come in handy to keep him in the dark about some things.

"I'll think about it," she agreed.

He lifted a careless hand and walked toward the stables, where he'd left his horse to be fed and groomed. All the way to the ranch he relived the passionate moments he'd just shared with Bernadette. And the memories made him wild for the ceremony to be over and done with . . . and all the guests on their way home.

He and Bernadette alone . . . .

Chapter Nine

THE WEDDING TOOK A MONTH TO ARRANGE. LUPE seemed to drag her feet deliberately, with a dozen excuses a day. Meanwhile, the old condessa worked on changing Eduardo's mind about his bride. She pointed out every flaw she could find with Bernadette, behind her back and to her face. The evenings when Bernadette and her father dined with Eduardo's family were pure torment.

Bernadette wondered how she was going to survive in the same house with that vicious old woman. She didn't dare criticize her to Eduardo. The camaraderie they'd been developing had all but disappeared. He grew more and more tense as the arrangements dragged on, and he didn't touch his intended bride at all, not even to give her a chaste kiss on the forehead. He kissed her hand, and not very enthusiastically at that. Bernadette worried that he'd lost all desire for her.

That wasn't the case at all. His desire had grown to violent proportions, so unmanageable that he was afraid to touch Bernadette lest it get away from him and dishonor them both. He was impatient with Lupe's delays and his grandmother's sarcastic comments, but he was determined not to let the women see that they were disturbing him. He only wanted the wedding over. Once he had Bernadette, the rest would work itself out.

Bernadette had wanted Maria to help dress her for the ceremony, in the large hotel in San Antonio where the wedding party was staying for the service at the huge and beautiful Cathedral of San Fernando. But the condessa had said that it would only be proper for Lupe to perform this honored task, and Eduardo, to save argument, had agreed. He wasn't in the best of humor because his friend who was to have stood for him as best man in the ceremony was ill and couldn't come. The man had cabled at the last minute, leaving Eduardo with no time to replace him.

Lupe wore the heaviest perfume she could find, and of course, Bernadette had an asthma attack that almost brought her to her knees. Eduardo, remembering what she'd said about the physician in New York, had her bags searched for the medication that had been prescribed and prayed that she'd had the foresight to bring it with her. She had.

He gave her the recommended dose himself from the little brown cork-stoppered bottle and cursed silently while it took effect.

"I'm so . . . sorry," Bernadette choked as she fought for each breath until the medicine worked.

"You have nothing to be sorry for," he said curtly. "I told Lupe—" He lowered his voice. "I told her about the perfume. She must have forgotten."

On purpose, Bernadette thought, and vowed revenge. But this wasn't the time, or the place. She lay back in the chair in her magnificent wedding gown and Eduardo held her hand, not speaking.

"Bad luck," she said after a minute, "for you to see me in my gown . . . before we're married."

"So they all say," he agreed. "I'm not superstitious. Nor should you be. Breathe slowly."

Bernadette thought how handsome he looked in his morning coat; he was the very picture of sartorial elegance. The white shirt complemented his dark complexion, and made his black eyes even more brilliant.

"You look so nice," she said.

He smiled. "And you do, too." He pursed his lips as he studied the amazing detail of the dress. "The gown is exquisite. From Paris?"

"Why, no," she replied and smiled gently. "From Madrid."

He was surprised.

"It was a model, from a new Spanish designer. I fell in love with it in the shop and had to have it."

"It suits your fairness."

"Thank you." She sat up slowly, able to breathe

a little more easily. "There. I'm better. I feel a little light-headed, but that's all."

He chuckled. "I will hold you up, if necessary."

She smiled at him, thinking about the wonderful life they were going to share as she let him help her to her feet.

Holding her gaze intently, he lowered the thin veil over her face. "The next time I look upon you," he said softly, "it will be when I lift this veil, and see you for the first time as my wife."

"I can hardly wait," she said huskily.

"Nor can I." He lifted her soft hands to his mouth and kissed it just above the knuckles. "Now, let us leave quickly, before any other misfortunes disrupt our plans!"

He hustled her out the door, past his stunned grandmother and cousin, and down the long staircase.

"You have broken tradition," the condessa grumbled as she followed along behind them. "It is bad luck for a man to see his bride in her finery!"

He turned and looked first at the condessa and then, angrily, at a subdued Lupe. "It is worse luck for the bride not to be able to appear at the ceremony. I told you," he chastised Lupe, "that heavy perfume would bring on an attack, did I not?"

Lupe clasped her hands tightly and tried to look dignified. "I forgot. I apologize most humbly."

"I think it would be best for you to start thinking about your return journey to Spain," he said unexpectedly. "I am certain," he added with a smooth smile, "that you would not want to impose upon a newly married couple."

Lupe went pale. The condessa actually gasped. "Eduardo, you forget to whom you speak!" she snapped with curt authority. "This American woman has bewitched you, that you would speak so rudely to a member of your own family!"

"Bernadette is more saint than witch. She will shortly be my wife," he added in a soft but menacing tone. "And I will expect her to be treated by my family with the courtesy that is her due. Come, Bernadette."

He escorted her outside to the waiting carriage. The patient driver inquired sincerely about her health, having been told the reason for the delay, and helped her into the carriage with Lupe and the condessa. Eduardo was to follow in another carriage, a separation that made Bernadette uneasy. Lupe was still saturated with perfume.

The door closed and the carriage began to move. The gloves came off at once. The condessa gave Bernadette a glare that would have felled a lesser woman.

"Of all the nonsense!" she exclaimed angrily. "That you should be the cause of such shame to Lupe!"

Bernadette, feeling much better from the effects of the medicine, smiled coldly at the old woman. "You may think that I am entirely ignorant of your mischief, but I am not quite so thick. You have done nothing for weeks but try to stop my marriage to Eduardo. You have schemed and plotted and behaved like a minion of the devil in pursuit of your own goals! You are a vicious and manipulative old woman who wants to order the lives of everyone around you. And you," she added, turning to Lupe as the condessa all but choked on her tongue, "are a rattlesnake masquerading as a woman! You knew that perfume would hurt my lungs, and you wore it deliberately. You are no better than that black scorpion beside you! Neither of you has any right whatsoever to treat Eduardo like a child to be pushed into marriage with a candidate of your choosing! He is a fine and honorable man! What a pity the same cannot be said for his family!"

"You brazen hussy!" the condessa cried in a high-pitched tone. "All of the county knows that you were out in the desert alone all night with my grandson! The servants whisper of it, they gossip! Your good reputation is ruined, and that is the only reason he is marrying you!"

Bernadette lifted her chin proudly, although the insult had made her cheeks pale. "Nothing happened in the desert that night that I would be ashamed for people to know about," she lied convincingly. "But it is not for that reason that Eduardo is marrying me, señora. He needs a substantial loan to repair the damage his mother did to the ranch, to keep it solvent. My father is the only hope he has of getting it."

The condessa was taken aback. "My grandson could come to me if he needed money," she snapped.

"He could. But why would he, when you would surely insist that he marry the pit viper beside you in order to acquire it?"

Lupe gasped. "How dare you!"

"Do not speak to her, Lupe," the condessa said harshly, trembling with impotent rage. "She is a shame and disgrace to all of us who are Cortes." She averted her eyes from Bernadette's wan features. "We shall not speak to her again. If Eduardo wants to ruin his life by marrying her, who are we to stop him?"

"How nice of you to see reason." Bernadette clenched her small posy of roses and baby's breath tightly in her hands and stared out the window. She had never felt so alone or so wounded, even by her father's insults.

The carriage arrived at the church where Bernadette's father awaited her at the curb. He helped her alight as if she truly was and always had been the most treasured of daughters. But as he peered at her through her veil, his beaming smile suddenly died. He glanced angrily at the two tight-lipped women who were being helped out of the carriage by the groomsmen.

"What's happened?" he asked his daughter as he led her into the huge cathedral.

"Nothing that I hadn't expected," she said quietly. "You can't imagine that they're happy to have him marry an American, can you? They wanted him to marry Lupe." She laughed miserably. "At least we've saved him from that fate worse than death!"

Her father's arm tightened under her hand. "Of all the cheek," he muttered furiously.

"This isn't the time," she said. "Eduardo can't help who he's related to."

"No, more's the pity. Buck up, lass," he added gently. "He won't let them hurt you."

"Oh, don't worry about me," she said gaily. "They're the ones who are going to need protection," she added, just loudly enough that the condessa and Lupe might hear. She saw them bristle visibly and it gave her the greatest satisfaction she'd had in the past several minutes.

The ceremony was elegant and beautiful. Despite the unpleasantness of its beginning, Bernadette was caught up in the wonder of being married, in the tradition of her own ancestors and of his. They knelt before the priest and the words were eloquent and timeless as he spoke them.

When Eduardo put the wedding ring on her finger, she felt tears washing down her cheeks. And when he lifted the veil and looked into her eyes, she thought that she'd never seen anything so beautiful as the tenderness in his black eyes as he saw her for the first time as his bride.

He caught his breath at the radiance in her face. He bent and his lips brushed hers reverently. He lifted his head and smiled. She smiled back. It was finished. They were man and wife.

On the return trip to the hotel for the reception Bernadette rode with Eduardo. She said nothing of the bitter conversation she'd had with his grandmother and Lupe, thinking that the less said, the sooner mended. Besides, she wanted to push away even the hint of a distressing thought and give free rein to her feelings of love for her new husband.

Bernadette changed from her wedding gown into a pretty green-and-white patterned party dress for the reception. She wove a matching green ribbon into her hair, braided it, and curled it around her head. She looked different, she thought as she surveyed herself in the mirror. She wasn't beautiful, but she looked radiant, as a bride should.

She tucked an embroidered silk handkerchief into her purse and went out into the hall, toward the staircase that would take her down to the room where the reception was being held.

But as she passed Eudardo's room, she paused. The door was ajar and she thought to join him so that they could go down together.

The sound of raised voices and a sobbing woman stopped her hand as she started to push the door open.

". . . cannot believe such a thing of her!" Eduardo was saying in Spanish.

"She laughed at Lupe," the condessa insisted, in that same tongue, obviously thinking that none of the guests understood the language so there was no danger of eavesdroppers. "She told Lupe that you had to marry her because of what you did together in the desert that night. She said that Lupe was a fool to hope that you could care for her, that she had bewitched you, and that you would toss Lupe and me aside if she asked you to. She said that we . . . that we would never see you again, that she would make sure of it!"

Why, the venomous old snake, Bernadette thought angrily. She started to go in, to confront the old woman with her blatant lie, when Eduardo spoke. His words froze her very heart.

"Bernadette has no voice in what I do at my own house with my own family," he said. "She will not distress you like this. My own grandmother."

Bernadette heard sniffling, but she couldn't determine if the crying came from the old woman or Lupe. She should have known they would try to punish her for the outburst in the carriage.

"I would have loaned you the money, Eduardo," the condessa said miserably. "I would have *given* you the money. Why did you not ask me? Why, instead, did you marry her?"

"Because you have done too much already," he replied tersely. "You raised me. You sent me to university. Everything I am, I owe to you. I will ask no more of you." He sighed heavily. "I could not marry Bernadette without being honest with her. I told her that I am not in love with her, but that I believe we will have a pleasant life together. And we shall. But you and Lupe will always be welcome here, whether or not she approves."

"Would her father not have loaned you the money without requiring you to marry her?" the condessa asked.

"He might have. But . . . well, there were other factors. And there was the gossip." He moved; Bernadette could hear his footsteps, followed by a long sigh.

"If only you had not kept her out all night and dishonored her, my grandson," the condessa said.

There was a harsh sound. "I did not dishonor her!"

"She accused you of doing just that!" Lupe inserted. "She bragged about it to us just as a hussy would."

"I would never have believed her capable of such a lie!" Eduardo said.

"She told everyone," Lupe invented, almost purring. "I have learned that the vaqueros did not spread the gossip, she spread it herself, to make sure that you would have to marry her."

Bernadette felt her heart contract. That was a master stroke of Lupe's, that lie. Eduardo would never believe now that Bernadette hadn't started the gossip. And it told her one other thing, that he'd thought of asking her father to make him a loan without the condition of marriage.

She stood there devastated. He had said there were dark places in his soul, and now she understood for the first time that it was those places that his grandmother and Lupe were adept at reaching. She was so numb that she didn't hear his footsteps moving toward the door until it was too late to escape.

He jerked the door open and saw Bernadette standing there. He didn't know that she spoke any Spanish, so he wiped the accusation from his features and composed himself to look as normal as possible.

"Bernadette," he greeted formally. "Shall we go downstairs?"

"Of course," She knew her voice sounded odd. She felt odd. She'd just been assassinated verbally and she couldn't do one thing about it. If Eduardo believed the lies of his grandmother and Lupe and did not even ask her for an explanation, what could she say that would sway him?

It was some sort of consolation that he didn't know her facility for his language. He would never know that she'd overheard the conversation. She'd been dreaming that he was falling in love with her, that he felt more for her than just desire, and was happy—actually happy—to be married to her. Now he was incensed because he believed she'd started the gossip about them—and lied to him.

"Out of the frying pan and into the fire," she muttered.

"I beg your pardon?" he asked politely.

She forced a smile to her lips. "Oh, nothing. I was only thinking out loud."

His black eyes narrowed. "How are your lungs?"

"They're fine."

"Lupe was genuinely sorry about the perfume. She asked me to convey her apologies to you."

She stopped and looked up at him. "The only regret Lupe has is that the perfume wasn't strong enough to bring on an attack that would kill me," she said, shocking him. "She and your grandmother hate me. They'll say or do anything that will break up our marriage. If you don't know that by now, you'll find it out sooner or later. But it will be too late," she added with quiet bitterness. "If I leave you, Eduardo, I won't come back. Not ever."

"This is an odd time to speak of leaving me, Señora Ramirez," he said coldly, using her married name as Americans would use it. In Spain, a woman kept her own family name, although her husband's was used in various ways.

"It's the last time I intend to speak of it," she

replied. She searched his eyes, seeing not what she wanted to see, but what was really there—resentment, disillusionment. She sighed. "I really was blind, you know. I was building castles in wet sand all the time." How could she have believed that the truce would last? There were those dark places in his soul; there was the fact that they had fought with each other for years.

He was scowling at her. "You make no sense."

She smiled sadly. "I know."

She followed his gaze as he looked around them, noticing that the guests were obviously waiting for the newlyweds to join the party in the reception room.

"Shall we go in?" Bernadette asked with forced gaiety. "I've tied my hair up so that it won't impede the axe."

"What?"

She didn't reply. She walked ahead of him, smiling at everyone, the very picture of happiness.

It was much later, when she said good-bye to her father and climbed into the carriage with Eduardo and the two hostile women, that she realized how she must act in the company of assassins.

She smoothed the skirt of her pretty dress and pulled her filmy shawl closer about her.

"It was a beautiful ceremony," Lupe told Eduardo. "A little long, I believe. But my arrangements were adequate, don't you think?"

"You did a wonderful job," Eduardo replied. He glanced at his wife. "Don't you agree, Bernadette?"

"Oh, everything was lovely," she said brightly. "And I did appreciate the many vases of pink roses. Fortunately, I had enough medicine to counteract the effects of the pollen."

Lupe bristled. "Flowers are necessary for any wedding," she said.

"Certainly they are, and Bernadette grows roses," Eduardo said.

Bernadette could have added that she spent a lot of time avoiding them when her garden was in full bloom. Eduardo knew that, too. He didn't want to admit that Lupe had gone out of her way to make it difficult for Bernadette at the altar.

"I was disappointed in the gown," Lupe continued coolly. "I would have gotten one from Madrid, instead of Paris. But I suppose the designers—"

"My gown *was* from Madrid," Bernadette interposed sweetly, "though purchased in New York."

The condessa tugged at her own shawl. "I had wondered," she said hesitantly. "The lace was very familiar."

"It should have been," Bernadette replied without meeting the other woman's eyes. "I understand that the lace I chose was used for generations by Cortes brides."

There was a faint intake of breath.

"You chose it for that reason?" Eduardo asked, surprised.

Bernadette averted her gaze to the darkness outside the swaying carriage. "It seemed appropriate to continue such a long-standing tradition."

There was a painful silence from the other side of the carriage. Neither of the woman spoke again until the carriage arrived at Rancho Escondido.

Lupe said good night with reluctance and obvious envy. The condessa followed suit, but her eyes didn't quite meet Bernadette's.

Eduardo led the way up the staircase and to the left, where the suite reserved for the married couple was located.

Bernadette had already decided that she wasn't going to share a room with him, when he opened a door that led into a bedroom done in a motif of white and pink with embroidered curtains and bedspread and canopy. It was so exquisitely feminine that she couldn't have imagined a man sharing it.

He noted her expression and nodded. "This will be your room," he said tightly, "for the duration of our marriage."

She lifted both eyebrows. "You have no interest in sharing one with me?" she prodded, knowing full well his reasoning and enjoying his discomfort.

His chin elevated and she saw his teeth clench.

"You said that you wanted me," she persisted. "Don't you anymore?"

His face was as bland as a rock. He stared at her and narrowed his dark eyes. "Tell me how the vaqueros knew that we spent the night together in the desert."

"I did tell you. Right after you arrived at my father's ball, but I'll be glad to remind you. The vaqueros knew because one of them overheard us talking to my father about it, of course."

"What if I say that I don't believe it, that I think you spread the story to make it impossible to back out of this marriage?"

"I offered to back out of that part of it, and so did my father."

He knew that, but what he'd heard from his family had warped his common sense. He glared at her. "Do you deny spreading the rumor?"

"I deny nothing," she replied coolly. "You must decide for yourself if I make a habit of lying."

He knew that she didn't. But, on the other hand, why would Lupe lie to him on this matter when he was beyond her reach as a prospective husband?

"And until you do decide," she continued, "I have no wish to sleep with you, so this arrangement suits me quite well."

His gaze went over her carelessly. "I hope you rest well, Senõra Ramirez. You will be called in time for breakfast."

How nice to look forward to another verbal

battle, she thought irritably. She glared at him as he walked back to the door. "How long are your relatives going to stay?"

"As long as they wish."

"I thought you told Lupe that she should pack?"

He stiffened. "She pleaded not to be sent away without my grandmother's company. I didn't have the heart to refuse her, especially after her sincere apology."

"Was it sincere? How nice."

"You make fun of her."

"Now, why should I wish to make fun of your cousin?" she asked reasonably. "Your family is unique. Your grandmother has the bearing of royalty and your cousin Lupe is as beautiful as an angel."

He scowled. "You don't like them."

"I don't know them. And I never will get the chance, because they hate the very sight of me," she added silently. But she smiled at her husband, hiding her misery and disappointment quite carefully from him. "I will visit my father from time to time, of course," she added. "And I would like to go and visit my brother soon, to tell him and my sister-in-law about the wedding. And to see their new baby."

"We will discuss this later," he said. "It is hardly appropriate for you to travel so far this soon after our wedding."

"Why ever not?" she asked innocently. "If your

family can camp here during our honeymoon, why can't I go and visit my brother?"

"Bernadette!" he said curtly.

She lifted her chin pertly. "Do you think it's appropriate to have a houseful of people wandering around here at such a . . . delicate time?"

His cheeks went ruddy with temper. "It will not be a delicate time!"

"Certainly not with an audience," she agreed. "But they aren't supposed to know that, are they? For all practical purposes, we're a newly married couple." She indicated the room. "And we're going to be living and sleeping apart, for all the household servants to see and gossip about." She smiled wider. "My, my, won't that look as if . . . well, you know how it will look."

It would look as if he wasn't capable of consummating the marriage, and he knew it. "If you continue this," he said slowly, "you may invite a situation that will be quite unpleasant for you."

"You mean you might ravish me?" she teased.

But he didn't smile, as he might have only weeks before. He looked cold and unapproachable—and insulted.

"A man does not ravish a wife." His gaze was cold. "At the beginning of all this, Bernadette, I told you our alliance would offer a mutual slaking of passions. At the moment however, you do not appeal to me in that light."

"How odd, given what you said the nights we were in the desert and in the pantry."

"A lady does not speak of such occasions."

"I'm not a lady," she replied. She smiled a little icily herself. "I'm the daughter of a railroad hand who built a fortune with his own hands."

"I've been a long time without a woman," he said finally. "You were willing and I lost my head."

"I see."

He sighed irritably, putting his hands behind him. "I won't invade your privacy and I'll expect you not to invade mine. We should get along well enough. As we discussed, you have a measure of independence and freedom here that you didn't have at home, and I will have a loan that was gained honorably, not through subterfuge and deception." His eyes narrowed. "I never pretended to love you, Bernadette. I have been honest."

"And I haven't?" she probed, trying to make him admit what had created this horrible situation between them.

He drew in a long breath. "God help me, I don't know." He turned away. He felt empty and betrayed . . . and confused.

"I'll stay here for two weeks," she told him. "If at the end of that time, your grandmother and Lupe are still here, I'm going to see my brother."

He whirled. "You think to dictate to me?"

She didn't back down an inch. "I'm telling you what I'm going to do," she replied with great dignity. "You think that your family wants nothing except your happiness. You're in for a rude awakening."

"I owe much to my grandmother," he said harshly. "She took me in when I had no one, she raised me, fed me, clothed me!"

"And made you aware every minute of your life that she'd done it," she fired right back. "Isn't that how she talked you into marrying Consuela?"

He took two long, angry strides toward her and caught her roughly by both arms. "You will never speak to me of Consuela!"

"Why, you're just like my father, aren't you?" she asked. "I thought class and position meant nothing to you, but they do. You're the outcast, the black sheep, the half-breed son of a Spanish nobleman and an American heiress with no morals. You want them to accept you, to approve of you, and you're willing to do anything that old woman asks you to do to prove that you're good enough to be a Ramirez!"

There was just enough truth in the accusation to make him livid. "Be quiet," he said harshly.

He was near the end of his control and she was pushing him right over it. She knew it and was excited by it.

"Wouldn't you do anything for your grandmother?" she persisted wildly. "Wouldn't you?"

"Bernadette . . ."

"She wants to tell you who to marry, where to

live, what to do with your life. Did she tell you when to make love to Consuela as well?"

"Make love?" he echoed, letting go of Bernadette only long enough to slam the door and lock it.

"You mustn't," she said huskily.

"I must. And I will."

Hours later, Eduardo left the room. Bernadette sat up. If only she could have accused him of rape! But it hadn't been. At first his hands had been rough, but once he bared her breasts and put his mouth on them, she was lost. One hot caress led to another, one kiss to a deeper next one, one intimate touch to an even more intimate touch that made her writhe with unexpected pleasure and plead for more.

She remembered that he'd laughed when she cried out to him in her blind search for fulfillment, that the hard thrust of him had lifted her right to heaven and all but sent her unconscious with the impact of so much sweet sensation. If there had been pain, she hardly recalled it through the hot throb of passion. Even in memory, her body began to swell and ache; how keenly aware she was now of her own capacity for pleasure, as well as Eduardo's skill at providing it. She hadn't imagined that she could let a man undress her and enjoy her body with all the lights blazing like this, or that she could be so brazen as to pull him down to her again even as they lay shivering in the aftermath of their first intimacy.

She lay down and stared at the ceiling, wondering at the violently passionate nature she shared with her husband.

Chapter Ten

BERNADETTE AWOKE FEELING VAGUELY ASHAMED. FOR so many years, the spectre of intimacy and its natural consequence, pregnancy, had frightened her almost to death. Then, last night, so suddenly, all her fears had vanished in the grip of an insane passion. She hadn't dreamed that she was capable of the sensations Eduardo's strong hands and warm mouth had given her. Nothing had penetrated that mist of sensual oblivion, least of all fear.

But now, she was truly a wife and there was every chance that she'd conceived. She touched her belly with curiosity and faint unease. If she was pregnant, would she survive? Was the New York physician correct in his assessment of her condition, that she could bear a child without dying in the process? He'd been right about her asthma. His unorthodox treatment had worked miracles. Exercise and fresh air were making a difference in her strength, and the medication he'd prescribed was helping her through the attacks. She flushed as she remembered the turmoil of the night before. She hadn't had any problem with her lungs—except for the breathlessness that must surely be a side effect of so much hungry passion in a man's arms.

She could barely think of it without catching her breath. Had Eduardo felt such pleasure as he'd given her? She had heard his harsh groan just at the last, when she was too exhausted to lift an arm around him. She remembered the convulsive shudder of his powerful body. Surely she, too, had groaned and shuddered when pleasure had consumed her totally. She closed her eyes and could see him above her, see the perfection of his lean body without clothing, see the maleness of him that was both frightening and exciting. She had known nothing of men and women in bed. Now she knew too much. It would have been better never to have experienced such passion, because now she would go hungry for it every night of her life. Eduardo was unlikely to come near her now, because she had made him very angry. But it hadn't lasted long, that anger. It had been transformed almost at once into an ardent, fiery passion that had exhausted both of them.

She pulled on her clothes and sat down gingerly at her vanity to brush her long, tangled blond hair. She looked different, although she wasn't sure exactly how. Her eyes held a new worldly wisdom, and her mouth had a softness that hadn't been there before. She wondered if it would be noticeable to the other occupants of the house—especially to her husband.

Once her hair was in its usual bun and she'd applied a trace of powder to her face, she went reluctantly down to face the rest of the household.

It was an anticlimax to find her husband was already gone. It was later than they usually breakfasted, however, so perhaps it wasn't unusual not to find him at the table. The condessa was there, and so was Lupe. They went right on talking as if she were invisible.

She was incensed at their duplicity. Her eyes narrowed as she poured coffee. "I trust you both slept well?" she asked coolly.

No one answered her.

She helped herself to sausages and eggs that she didn't really want, just to appear normal. "I slept quite well," she said. "When I finally slept," she added with a wicked glance toward them.

The condessa was outraged. She put down her utensil with a thud. "Decent women do not speak of such things, especially at the table!"

"But I'm not a decent woman," Bernadette replied calmly. "At least, that's what you told my husband. You led him to believe that I started gossip that ensured he would marry me."

Lupe glared at her with singular fury. "It was he who said it," she replied.

"You lie," Bernadette returned shortly. "You said it. And more besides."

Lupe cast down her napkin and got up to storm from the room.

The condessa remained, less hostile than she had been a minute before. She studied Bernadette carefully, her hand resting on the delicate china cup which contained her sweetened coffee.

"Hablás español," she said. It was a statement. She knew that Bernadette spoke Spanish, had to speak it, or she could never have understood what was said in Eduardo's room just after the wedding.

"As well as you speak English," Bernadette conceded.

The condessa was less sure of herself now. She studied the other woman with open curiosity. "Why did you say nothing?"

"I would not for worlds attempt to gain my husband's respect now by admitting that I understand his language. He has accepted as fact that I went out of my way to antagonize you and Lupe, that I lied and spread gossip. He admitted to you," she added painfully, because it hurt to remember, "that he has no love for me." She lifted her face proudly. "Well, the marriage is an accomplished fact and divorce is impossible. We must all make the best of it." She sipped her coffee and put the cup back down. "I am not what you wished for in a granddaughter-in-law, but I have more humanity than did your precious Consuela, who treated Eduardo like a monster."

The intake of the old woman's breath was audible.

"You didn't know?" Bernadette asked coldly. "Oh, I see, you only manipulate other people, you don't bother with learning the consequences of your meddling. You never saw Eduardo after the loss of his wife and son, but I did."

The condessa put a hand to her throat.

"He never would have told you all he went through with Consuela, the loss of the child," Bernadette said bitterly. "He loves you too much to burden you with it."

The condessa lowered her eyes to the table and touched, gently, the handle of the china cup. "You did not believe him a murderer."

"No," she replied coldly.

"Why?"

"Because I love him!" Bernadette said with barely concealed anguish. She met the old woman's shocked eyes evenly. "I love him more than my own life," she said in a rough whisper. "Enough to bear any gossip, any censure, to be near him. He asked me to marry him, and even though I knew it was only because he needed my father's money, I couldn't agree quickly enough. I hoped . . ." Her eyes closed as she fought for self-control. "I hoped so desperately that he might one day come to care for me, just a little. But I see now, for myself, what a forlorn, desperate hope it was." Her eyes opened, misty with pain. "I was a fool. I should have refused to marry him the day I met you and Lupe. I should have known that I couldn't fight the two of you. Eduardo owes you loyalty and love. He would never disbelieve anything you told him." She put down her napkin and got to her feet. "And of course, you would never lie to him, because you love him and wish only for his happiness," she added with faint sarcasm, pleased when the old woman actually flushed. "That's what he said to me last night. That I had no honor because I accused you of telling a lie and backing up Lupe's lie." She pushed her chair back under the table with hands that trembled. "But it is not I who lack honor, Señora Condessa. It is you. I curse the day I met you."

She turned and started toward the door.

"You are a brazen woman!" the condessa said in a shaky tone. "My grandson would be well rid of you, as his father would have been well rid of his mother!"

Bernadette had had quite enough of that holier-than-thou attitude. She walked back to the table, lifted the cream pitcher, and poured its contents right over the old woman's immaculate hair.

"Cream for kitty cat," Bernadette said haughtily, and left the sputtering old woman sitting there in the mess.

* * *

She didn't know where Eduardo was, and she didn't care. She was furious enough to pack her bags and leave. Which is exactly what she did. She took the suitcase to the front porch herself, shocking the servants and outraging Lupe, who came out into the hall and saw what she was up to.

"What are you doing!" Lupe exclaimed.

"Leaving," Bernadette said through her teeth. "You and the condessa are welcome to my husband, who obviously has more feeling for you than he can manage to pretend for me."

"But it is the day after the wedding!" Lupe cried. "You will disgrace him!"

"Do you think so?" Bernadette asked with mock delight. "Imagine how the servants will gossip when they change the sheets in my bedroom!" she added for good measure, smiling when Lupe almost swooned at the crude remark. "They'll think that he wasn't up to my expectations," she added wickedly.

Lupe looked as if she might faint. Bernadette walked right around her and back to her room to get her shawl and purse. She cast one last look at the rumpled bed and laughed coldly to herself. So much for her brief taste of married life. She would never be tricked into a man's clutches again.

She walked back to the front porch, where the servant she'd charged to hitch up the buggy was waiting with a pained expression. Lupe had obviously tried to forbid him to leave the ranch.

"Never you mind," Bernadette told him in perfect Spanish. "No one will blame you for this. It is my order, which you cannot disobey. All right?"

"Sí, señora," he replied gratefully.

Bernadette allowed him to help her into the buggy after he'd loaded her case. "I'll send for the rest of my things," she told Lupe. "You can tell Eduardo whatever lie you like, I'm sure he'll swallow anything now. Good-bye."

She nodded to him and he flicked the whip above the horse's head, putting the buggy in motion.

All the way home, Bernadette grieved for what might have been. She no longer cared what Eduardo thought or did. She was going to put him right out of her mind and go visit her brother, as she'd threatened. Eduardo could do what he liked.

Her father met her at the front door, morose and unhappy when he saw her expression.

"Sure and I never should have let you go there in the first place, lass," he said through his teeth as he helped her down and waited for the servant to bring her bag before he gave the boy a tip and sent him home.

"He should have married Lupe," she said. "And that's all I want to say about it. I won't burden you by staying here any longer than I have to," she added with frigid pride. "I'll go to Albert as soon as I can get a ticket on the next train."

"Oh, lass, no, you're not a burden," her father said sadly. "You're welcome here as long as you want to stay. I'm sorry for the whole miserable mess I've caused with my misplaced ambitions. Lass, I wouldn't have wished that cold lot on you for all the world. I've hardly slept thinking about the treatment you've had from that old woman and that Lupe."

Her father's concern warmed her heart. It was so nice to have a relative care about her well-being for a change, especially this man, who'd never concerned himself very much with her feelings at all.

"Thank you, Father. I must say, I've hardly slept myself," Bernadette added without saying why. "I want to rest. Then I really do want to go see Albert. I think it would do me good to go away for a while."

"In a few days," he agreed. "Once you've gotten over the ordeal."

A few days. A few weeks. What did it matter? Nothing was going to change the sad path of her life now. Married and discarded in less than a day, they'd say, and they'd be right. Nobody would blame the condessa or Lupe, they'd blame Bernadette. It was her lack of breeding, they'd say, that led to such a disastrous end to the marriage. Eduardo would still have his loan, because that had already been settled and paid. Her father was too honorable a man to call back the money now. And if Eduardo was willing to lie, perhaps he could have the marriage annulled. Then he could marry pretty Lupe and stand to inherit his grandmother's fortune. How wonderful for him!

But Bernadette's hopes were as dead as her dreams. It was all she could do to keep from bawling her eyes out. Eduardo had been so different before the arrival of his kinfolk. Bernadette mourned the death of the beautiful relationship that had been building between them.

She wondered if he'd even be upset when he returned home and found her gone. She seriously doubted it. The condessa would be furious at Bernadette's treatment of her and was bound to want revenge. So would Lupe. Eduardo would believe anything they told him. And probably he wouldn't care that she'd left. He hadn't even spoken to her when he'd left her bed. That had hurt most of all.

She went to her old room and settled down on the comfortable daybed by the window. In minutes, despite her misery and some coughing from the dust on the way home, she was sound asleep.

It was well after dark when Eduardo dismounted at the stable and walked quickly toward the house. His conscience was flaying him over the way he'd treated Bernadette. Not that he'd hurt her, because he knew he hadn't. But he'd used her like a woman of the streets, and all because she'd made him angry with her accusations. It was dishonorable behavior at best. He was ashamed to face her.

His grandmother and Lupe were in the parlor when he arrived, both involved in their endless needlework. He remembered that Bernadette was skilled at embroidery, but apparently she hadn't been asked to join the women tonight.

"Where is Bernadette?" he asked curtly.

"Resting," his grandmother said, throwing Lupe a speaking glance. "She is resting. She said that she wished not to be disturbed, so we have not disturbed her."

He relaxed a little. That was good news. At least she hadn't packed her bags and left, which was what he'd truly expected. Perhaps her pride wasn't as lacerated as he imagined it was.

"Have you eaten?"

"No." The condessa got gracefully to her feet and put a gentle hand on Eduardo's arm. "We waited for you, my boy. You must be very tired."

"I am. And very hungry. What about Bernadette?"

"She had a tray earlier."

They went in to dinner. His grandmother reminisced; Lupe flirted with him and made him laugh; he allowed himself to be diverted.

He paused at Bernadette's room on his way to bed, but there was no light peeking from under the door and he heard no sound, so he assumed that she was asleep. It was just as well, he thought, not to have any more words with her now. Tomorrow, when they were both calmer, they could talk about what had happened, and what sort of future they could build on the damaged foundation of their marriage.

He'd put the money her father had loaned him to good use so far. Equipment was being bought, the house was being painted, bad wood was being replaced, and the livestock was being added. His prospects were better than they'd ever been, and he owed all that to his new father-in-law. He would pay back the loan, he promised himself. And perhaps he could help Bernadette salvage some of her lost pride. He found her incredibly attractive. He wanted her, more than ever, since their sweet, hot night of passion. He could overlook what she'd done and said. He could start again. They could have a good life together. She could keep his books and help him to rebuild Rancho Escondido, and the future would be pleasant.

He said as much to his grandmother at breakfast. She seemed uneasy and Lupe looked as if she'd swallowed a melon whole. The two of them acted guilty.

His suspicions grew by the minute as breakfast finished and still there was no sign of his new bride. He finished his coffee and fixed suspicious eyes on them. "Where is Bernadette?" he demanded.

Lupe actually jumped. The condessa lifted her head in a regal angle. "She has gone to her father," she said coolly. "Where she belongs. She was never of a social class to belong in this great house, and she is not fit to be a wife to you. It is better that the marriage be annulled at once. Then, perhaps, you might marry Lupe." She smiled at her niece. "She has an excellent background and is quite healthy. With her family's wealth, and mine, you could found an empire together in Spain. For certainly, you would inherit when I die, if you married her."

"And what of Luis?" he asked, his voice barely audible as he controlled it.

"Luis?" she waved her frail hand. "Luis has the vineyards and his wife's property."

Eduardo put his napkin down with deliberate care. "Did you not offer him marriage to Lupe before he announced his betrothal to Carisa Morales?"

The condessa frowned. "Yes. But, of course, he was not good enough for Lupe," she added quickly. "Is that not so, my dear?"

Lupe started to answer, but Eduardo's black eyes burned into her face and silenced her.

"When did Bernadette go home, Abuela?" he asked quietly.

The old woman toyed with her napkin. "Last evening, I believe."

"Last evening!" he exploded. "You told me she was upstairs!"

The condessa looked vaguely distressed. "You were tired, my dear. I thought it just as well not to upset you. I told Lupe, and she agreed that it was better to say nothing until you were morc . . . rested."

He stood up, his bearing autocratic and menacing. "Bernadette went home alone, in the dark, is this what you are saying?"

"It was still light," Lupe replied quickly.

"Ay, Dios." He breathed harshly. "That long ago, and I knew nothing of it."

"She is a vicious girl!" the condessa said with equal harshness. "She poured a pitcher of cream over my head!"

Eduardo gaped at her. "What?"

"She did!" Lupe said. "Your poor grandmother, she might have caught a chill! I had to fetch a servant to clean up the mess! How can you wish to remain the husband of such a savage woman?"

Both his eyebrows lifted. He was staring as if he didn't recognize either of them.

"Why did she pour cream on you, Abuela?" he asked.

The old woman frowned. "We were arguing. She simply lost her temper."

"She would never attack without provocation. So what did you say to her?"

The old woman glowered. "She said that she

was going home and that you deserved no better than the company of Lupe and myself. She said that we were creatures without honor."

He was beginning to wonder about that, himself. His black eyes narrowed. "And you said . . . ?" he prompted.

She sucked in a breath. "I said that you would be well rid of her!"

"Why?"

She colored red. Her eyes averted. "She said . . ."

"Yes?"

She swallowed and lowered her eyes. "She told Lupe that she would leave deliberately, so that the servants would gossip about it. So that they would say that you did not live up to her . . . expectations!"

He threw back his head and laughed. It was the first bit of amusement he'd felt in such a long time. He could picture Bernadette throwing cream over his grandmother, blatantly accusing Eduardo of disappointing her in bed, and leaving him to face the renewed gossip about his prowess. He should be furious, but he wasn't. Bernadette had neatly turned the tables on his grandmother, and he was filled with admiration for her. He was beginning to get a very clear picture of what was going on in his house. He'd been blind in every way, it seemed.

"It is not amusing!" his grandmother said furiously.

"Yes, it is," he returned. He smiled down at her.

"You are my family, and I love you very much. But you have been most unfair to Bernadette, who never meant you any harm. Her life has been a very difficult one. Her father blamed her for the death of her mother in childbirth. He has treated her like a burden for all these years. In a sense she married me to escape him. And you have sent her back into the fire."

The condessa averted her eyes. "She is uncivilized."

"She is spirited and independent," he corrected. "She is the sort of woman who will stand beside a man and fight the world with him and for him. Sadly, it will not be me," he added, surprised to find that it disturbed him to know that. "You should have given her a chance. So should I have," he added quietly.

His grandmother waved her hand. "It is done," she said. "She has gone and I think she will not come back."

"We will see." He bent to kiss his grandmother's solemn face gently. "You care for me, in your way, but you have no idea what sort of man I am, or what sort of wife I require. You made a disastrous choice in Consuela, and I never told you for fear of hurting your feelings. I should have been less caring and more honest. Consuela hated this place and hated me. Her hatred turned her into a cold, bitter woman. She became demented, turned her back on her own baby and let him starve to death," he said harshly.

The condessa's face went white. "No!"

"Yes," he affirmed. "I came home and found him in his cradle. She had dismissed the servants. She was sitting in the parlor doing her needlepoint as if nothing in the world was wrong. When I told her about the child, she simply looked at me with a total lack of comprehension or guilt. Two days later, just after the funeral, she took one of my guns and walked up into the mountains behind the house. We found her hours later, with a bullet through her head." His gaze fell to the floor. "There was much gossip afterward. At least a few people thought that I blamed her for the death of the child and killed her in revenge." His head lifted proudly. "It was not the truth. In fact, Consuela went mad after the birth of the child and was no longer competent to be either wife or mother. I had servants with her all the time. But when I left that once, on a business trip, she dismissed them and there was no one to reason with her about the child. She hated me, she said, for the attention I paid the child. She made sure that I would never pay him attention again."

The condessa put her face in her wrinkled old hands and wept.

Eduardo touched her shoulder lightly, his mind still locked into the pain of the past. "I drank to excess afterward, more for grief of the child than her.

I would have died on one binge, I think, except that Bernadette braved the pistol in my hand and came and took it away from me. She brought me back to life again, made me see that I could not die with the child and Consuela. She saved me, in her ever so careful, subtle way. I never knew why."

The condessa did, and it made her guilt all the more damning. She'd known none of these details. She looked up at her grandson through layers of guilt and regret and knew that nothing she did would make up for what she'd cost him.

Lupe, who'd been silent all this time, went forward to take the old woman's hands and draw her up out of the chair. "You should rest, Tía," she said gently. She glanced up at Eduardo's hard face. Regret was in her eyes, too, along with a helpless attraction that all the long years hadn't erased. She shrugged. "Perhaps we are both at fault for Bernadette's flight," she said. She stiffened her spine a little. "If you ask her to come back, she will not have cause for further complaint," she added. "From me, or from Tía. I give you my word."

Eduardo sighed. "I fear that it will take more than that to entice her here again," he replied, thinking not of their behavior, but of his own. Bernadette would not easily forget how he had humbled her. And, too, there were possible consequences of that action that would terrify her. He grimaced as he remembered the death of her mother and her sister in childbirth. She would be frightened and her father would do nothing to comfort her. She would be alone, as she always had been, except when she'd been with him. He would give anything at that moment to go back to the days when she trusted him, when she cared for him. How she must hate him now!

He watched the condessa go along to the staircase with Lupe, and he thought how old she looked, how alone. She had no life of her own left. Her only pleasure was in manipulating the lives of the people around her. This arrogance had led to the greatest tragedy in his life, and she'd never known. Now that she did, perhaps her arrogance would fade away and she would become the kind and gentle woman of his childhood. . . .

Despite the early hour, Eduardo saddled a horse and rode to the Barron ranch. He didn't expect Bernadette to want to see him, but he had to make the attempt for the sake of his honor. He'd caused enough problems for this child-woman in his fashion. Now he had to try and make amends.

He rode up to the house, dismounted, and tied the reins to the hitching post. Maria met him at the front door with a worried frown.

"¿Qué pasa?" he asked at once, because he knew from her expression that something was terribly wrong here.

"It is the señorita . . . the señora," she corrected at once, then grimaced. "Perhaps it was the ride home in the wind and dust yesterday, who knows? She awoke the household last night, it was such a vicious attack of the lungs. She is very bad. The medicine has not worked. Señor Barron has sent for the doctor." She shook her head and looked at him through tears. "We think . . . she may die, señor!"

Chapter Eleven

EDUARDO ENTERED BERNADETTE'S ROOM WITH TERROR in his heart. He couldn't remember feeling so afraid and miserable—except when he had found his young son dead.

Colston Barron was sitting beside the bed where a white, still Bernadette lay trying to get a breath. She was propped up, pale and sweating. Her breathing was audible, raspy . . . horrible.

Eduardo went close to the bed and looked down at her over the head of her father. "The medicine," he said urgently. "Have you used the medicine?"

Colston looked at him blankly. "Coffee, sure," he said dully, "and some of that herbal tea that Dr. Blakely gave her—"

"No!" he interrupted quickly. "The medicine she brought home from New York!"

Colston still didn't quite grasp what the younger man was saying. "Oh, that. We couldn't find it. It's not in the bag she brought home."

"Mother of God," Eduardo said, shaken. "I'll be back as soon as I possibly can!"

He rushed to the front of the house, untied his mount's reins, leapt into the saddle, and all but killed the horse getting back to Rancho Escondido. He vaulted out of the saddle at the front door, yelling for a stable boy to bring him a fresh horse.

Taking the steps two at a time, he refused to remember what he'd seen, lest the terror delay him even longer from his purpose. He went to the room Bernadette had occupied and began rummaging through her trunk until he found the precious vial of medicine.

"Eduardo," Lupe exclaimed when he rushed past her in the hall. "What is wrong?"

"Bernadette is dying," he said through his teeth, and kept going.

Lupe, startled, barely heard the exclamation from the tiny old woman standing just inside her own doorway.

"Dying, did he say?" the condessa exclaimed.

"Her medicine," Lupe murmured. "He must have come home for it. She left it behind." She turned back to the condessa. "She must not have been thinking clearly," she said, unsettled.

The condessa crossed herself. "God forgive me," she whispered, and turned away.

Eduardo rode back the way he'd come, the medicine tight in one hand the entire ride. Dear God, please, he prayed, let me be in time!

The trip seemed to take forever. He was aware of

every cloud in the sky, the sound of dogs baying somewhere nearby. He felt the threat of rain in the air, but none of these things really made any impression on his tortured mind. All he could see, think, breathe was Bernadette. He had to be in time.

He took the last lap up to the house apologizing to the poor horse, so exhausted that it could barely breathe. He left it at the front porch and ran inside, down the hall to Bernadette's room. The raspy sound of her breathing filled the space. Her face was white and cold, but sweating just the same. He could see her breaths at the base of her throat, could see her ribs expanding as she tried to get oxygen into her lungs, past the stale air she couldn't force out of them.

Colston stood up when he saw what Eduardo had in his hand. "*That* medicine," he said absently, and his eyes were red. He wiped at one eye with his sleeve. "I never even thought of it."

"She left it behind." Eduardo moved forward, measured the dose, and lifted Bernadette's head gently to administer it. "Here," he whispered. "Here, Bernadette, you must take it. This is your medicine. It will ease the spasm so that you can breathe. Come, open your mouth, querida."

She remembered very little since her arrival home. Eduardo was here, she could barely make him out through her tortured eyes. He was trying to give her something. What was it? She obeyed his deep voice mechanically and took the medicine.

Eduardo took Colston's place by the bed then and waited, cradling Bernadette's small hand closely in his. He was holding her right hand, but he noticed the left, lying on her chest. There was no ring on it. He winced, because he knew to his cost why the ring was missing. She'd taken it off. She'd taken him out of her life. He deserved it, but it hurt.

"That medicine," Colston said, "it worked before. Do you think it will work this time? She's so bad, Eduardo, so bad!"

"It will work," he said doggedly. "It must work!" He wouldn't let himself believe otherwise. Bernadette couldn't die. He couldn't lose her. Life would be worthless without her.

His fingers tightened around hers. Was he imagining it, or was her breathing a little less labored now? He stood up and moved closer to her, so that he could see her face more clearly. Yes, she was relaxing. Her eyes opened as she breathed. Her whole chest heaved violently with the struggle to catch each breath. The hollow at the base of her throat sucked in with each pull of air. He could see the paleness of her face, the cold sweat that covered it. She was in agony, and he wanted to bear the pain for her.

Her mouth opened, but she couldn't get words out. She sat up a little more, bending forward. The medicine was making her head spin. But her chest was relaxing. Her lungs were relaxing.

She slowly inhaled . . . and the air came out again! She laughed softly at the sudden ease of breathing. She did it again. Then again.

"She's breathing easier, do you see, lad?" Colston exclaimed. "Praise God!"

"Praise Him, indeed," Eduardo said heavily. "Bernadette, is it easing now?"

"Yes," she managed huskily. "It's . . . better."

He drew her forehead to his chest and held it there, bending over it with eyes that stung from sudden moisture. "You little fool!" he exploded against her soft hair, holding her head even closer as the anguish he'd kept at bay for the past horrifying hour washed over him and made him shake inside. "You little fool, you could have died, coming away without your medicine!"

"What . . . do you care?" she retorted. "You . . . never even bothered . . . to come after me!"

His hands loosened a bit. He lifted his head from her hair and moved back a little. "Bernadette, I didn't know that you weren't in your room until this morning," he said miserably. But he could tell she didn't believe him. She looked at him with cold green eyes. He winced. Her feelings did not stem alone from him not coming after her but from what he'd done to her on their wedding night.

She lay back down against the high pillows and

sucked in fresh air. Her eyes closed at the effort and then opened again. It was easier to breathe, but still uncomfortable.

"Thank you for fetching the medicine," Colston said with heartfelt emotion as he clapped the younger man on the back. "I was so afraid for her. She said to get her the medicine, and I thought she meant that herbal tea, curse me slow brain!"

Bernadette had been surprised by her father's care of her, a new and unusual occupation for him. She'd been even more surprised by Eduardo's arrival and his rush to obtain her medicine from her trunk. She hadn't remembered that it was in the trunk and not her suitcase. It was almost a fatal error.

"Would you like some fresh coffee, girl?" her father asked gently.

She nodded slowly.

"I'll fetch it from Maria. Be right back!"

He went out and Eduardo sat down in the chair he'd occupied, close by Bernadette's side.

"Why are you . . . here?" she asked, averting her embarrassed face. "Haven't you done enough?"

He felt his face heat with the remark. He stared at his hands while he searched for something to say that would alleviate the hurt he'd dealt her. "I lost myself the night of our wedding," he said quietly. "Absolutely. I have no excuse to offer except that I was angry and had no control over my temper and my passions. I realize that what . . .

happened . . . was difficult for you. I apologize most humbly for my treatment of you. I apologize for believing you lied to me."

She flushed at the memory. She couldn't bear to meet his searching gaze with the incident between them. He knew her body as no one knew it, how it looked and felt and reacted to his practiced caresses. She had begged him. . . .

Her faint moan of embarrassment went right through his body like a hot arrow. "Forgive me," he said heavily. "You were a virgin. I had no right to treat you that way, so crudely. I have no real excuse," he added quietly, lifting his dark eyes back to her face, "except that I wanted you so desperately that it was impossible for me to draw back."

She colored even more. Her hands gripped the bedspread and she averted her face.

"Ah, I can see the shame," he remarked gently. "You remember not so much what I did as how you behaved with me, is that not the real problem?"

"Please," she choked. "I can't . . . speak of it!"

"We must," he replied. He reached for her hand and clasped it gently in his. "Bernadette, you are my wife," he added softly. "What I did with you happens between men and women. It is part of marriage."

She bit her lower lip to stop its trembling, but tears washed her eyes. "I behaved like a woman from a brothel."

His hands tightened on hers. "You behaved like a woman who very badly wanted to belong to the man she married," he said in a voice that reached only her ears, that wouldn't have carried to the doorway. "How exquisite was our loving, Bernadette. How passionate." He lifted her hand to his mouth, turned it, and kissed the damp palm hungrily. "I could not face you afterward for the shame and self-contempt I felt. I meant to force you. You knew this, of course?"

She nodded jerkily. "But you didn't . . . force me."

"No. You were generous. More generous than I deserved." He drew in a long breath. "Everything has gone wrong with us. I had such high hopes for our marriage, and I have done nothing but kill them. I want you to come back with me."

She shook her head.

His fingers caressed hers. "My grandmother has promised that she will cause no more trouble between us," he coaxed. "So has Lupe."

"I should rather leap into a pit of vipers!"

He smiled ruefully. "An apt description, I fear, but they are my family, however unpleasant." He moved closer, searching her green eyes. "Come home," he whispered. "I will love you again, but more slowly, more tenderly, so that I create an addiction you can never satisfy."

Her body tingled. She glowered at him, blushing scarlet. "Don't you talk to me that way!"

He smiled wickedly and kissed her knuckles warmly. "I want to do much more than talk," he whispered, letting his eyes drop to her breasts and caress them. "Dios mio, what it cost me to leave you after our lovemaking! I looked at you and ached to my very toes."

"You didn't even speak to me!"

He shrugged in a very Spanish way and smiled. "I left you out of shame."

She stared at his lean, beautiful hands and remembered their tenderness, their mastery on her body. She drew in a longer, slower breath. "I was ashamed, too," she said quietly. "Of the things I said to you." Her voice broke.

His mouth burned against her fingers. "Wicked, wonderful things," he whispered. "They brought my blood up, made me reckless and wild with you, excited me! I enjoyed the things you said to me, querida, so much that I said them back to you. Have you forgotten?"

No, she hadn't, and her whole body tingled at the thought. She lifted her face and searched his black eyes. They were tender and full of affection. It had been so long since he'd smiled at her in that particular way.

His teeth nipped the skin on the back of her hand affectionately. His face tautened. "You looked at me as I poised just above you. When you saw me for the first time like that, you gasped."

She'd gasped even more at what came next, at

the tender parting of her long legs, at the slow, measured thrust of his body down into hers and the shock of intimacy, real intimacy, that had accompanied it.

"I hurt you a little," he whispered, staring right into her eyes, "and you gasped again. But you were too hungry for me to ask me to stop. You lifted, so that I could enter you more easily . . ."

"Eduardo!"

"And you watched as I did it," he continued sensually. He smiled at her embarrassment. "That intensified our pleasure, the watching. It was wicked, was it not? Wicked and satisfying all at once."

She swallowed. "You . . . you said that you'd never let a woman see you."

"Nor had I." His fingers traced the lines in her palm. "Such intimacy was a thing I could do only in darkness, because I felt a sort of shame with the women I . . . mastered." He glanced down at the small fingers held in his. "With Consuela—well, I told you how that was." He met her soft eyes. "I never knew that sex could be such a poignant thing, such a reverent thing, as we shared together in the light. You gave me true ecstasy, fulfillment far beyond anything I had ever experienced before, and I was shaken. I was unsettled by the experience and I felt guilty that I had all but forced you to submit to me. For that, too, I am sorry. My lack of perception almost cost you your life."

She studied him with new insight. He was a complex man. He kept his deeper feelings carefully hidden, but they were there. He had to care something for her to have made such a fuss over her medicine.

"And you," he continued softly, "achieved satisfaction, too, did you not, Señora Ramirez?"

She dropped her gaze like a hot rock and her breathing became ragged again.

"Here, now, none of that," he chided, lifting her chin so that he could see her eyes. "In this most intimate of married affairs, we must never hide the truth from each other. I satisfied you completely?"

She swallowed hard. "Yes," she whispered.

He nodded. "But there was pain."

"A . . . a little."

"Yes. You bled."

She colored and averted her eyes.

"That, too, is natural," he told her. "I did not damage you. The wound will heal and it will never be uncomfortable for you again."

She let out the breath caught in her throat. "It embarrasses me to speak of these things."

"You are my wife. Come home and live with me."

She looked at him warily. "Why?"

He smiled. "Because a woman who feels sufficiently confident to pour cream over the head of the condessa is the sort of wife I require to help me save Rancho Escondido."

She grimaced. "I shouldn't have done that, not

even after what she said to me," she murmured. "It was horrible to treat a helpless old woman in such a way."

"Helpless? Abuela?" He put a hand to her forehead. "You must have a fever if you believe that. Abuela will not be helpless on her deathbed. She, too, has regrets. Come back and let her apologize." His white teeth glinted. "It will be a once-in-a-lifetime opportunity, I assure you. And even as she performs this interesting and profound new exercise, I am certain she will find a way to make herself sound guiltless."

Bernadette managed to laugh. She searched his face. "And Lupe?"

He brought her hand to his knee and held it there. "Lupe is my cousin. Nothing more. She would never have been anything more. I know she feels a tenderness for me, but I am incapable of returning it," he said simply. "I want you. Only you, Bernadette."

And she wanted him. But she was too insecure to say so. She lay breathing softly, her eyelids drooping as the sedative took full effect.

"Will you?" he asked gently.

"Will I stay in a room of my own?"

He drew in a long breath. "Yes. Of course. You will have whatever you wish."

Whatever she wished. She glanced toward the window, where blue sky and fluffy white clouds were visible through the thin fabric. "I must think about it."

He hesitated. It was a tricky time. He had to be careful not to upset her anymore than he already had. He looked down at her small hand with its neatly rounded fingernails. "It would please me more if you slept with me," he added quietly. "But I understand how you must feel."

She was surprised. "You . . . still want me?"

Her question, as much as her tone, surprised him. He lifted his gaze back to her face. She had more color now, and her green eyes were sparkling. "That never stops," he said quietly.

"But you just said I'd stay in a separate room . . . !"

"Only because it was what I thought you wanted," he replied shortly. "Dear God, Bernadette, I took you like you were a woman of the streets! How could I expect you to want me again, after that?"

Her eyes widened. "You did?"

Her innocence made him feel ancient. He laughed in spite of the gravity of the situation. "What a shameless question. Do you really expect me to answer it?"

She glanced toward the doorway, but there was no one there, and no approaching footsteps, either. She leaned forward earnestly. "*Is* that how a man does it with a . . . with a bad woman?" she whispered.

"Bernadette!" He laughed helplessly. "My God!"

"Well, if it is," she continued, unabashed, "how . . . how is it supposed to be with a girl who isn't bad?"

He took the question at face value and answered it the same way. "Tender," he replied. "Without the urgent handling and insistent kisses. Without the violence of penetration and the hard rhythm."

She colored prettily. "But . . ."

"But what?"

"But that was why it was so . . . exciting."

He nodded. "For me, too," he confessed. "It was the best lovemaking I ever had. But I should have been more careful with you. It was your first experience of a man."

"It was all I hoped it would be," she told him. "And very embarrassing! In the light, I mean!"

He sighed softly. "That was the only thing I did right," he told her. "I loved you in the light, so that I saw your face at the moment you became my lover, my woman, my wife. I can hold that expression of awe and pleasure in my heart until I am a very old man. I would not have missed it for the world."

She was surprised. Embarrassed, certainly, but pleased as well. "I couldn't see you at all," she whispered. "Your face blurred. I felt as if I might die from the pleasure, it was so strong."

He smiled. "You flatter me."

"I wouldn't know how."

He chuckled. "You do now." He leaned closer. "There are even more shocks in store for you, too, Señora Ramirez."

She smiled self-consciously. "Are there, really?"

What he might have said then was a moot point, because her father and Maria came into the room each with a tray laden with coffee and cake.

"So much better!" Maria exclaimed when she saw the color in Bernadette's face. "Praise the Virgin, what a miracle el conde worked!"

"A miracle, indeed," Colston said with quiet gratitude. "You saved her life."

"Appropriate," he replied, watching Bernadette sip black coffee. "I think she saved mine, once."

Bernadette frowned slightly. "I did?"

"Soon after the death of my wife and son," he reminded her. "I got drunk and was waving a pistol around, have you forgotten?"

She shook her head. "I thought you might be thinking of shooting someone with it."

"I was," he said with grim humor. "Myself."

"No!"

His broad shoulders rose and fell. "It was a difficult time for me. I found the child, you see, dead of . . ." He glanced up and saw Colston Barron hesitating, as if he were about to leave the room.

"Come and sit down, Colston," Eduardo said heavily. "The two of you were the only champions I had during that terrible time. I never spoke of what happened. I think I should. I would like you both to know the truth."

Colston still hesitated. "My boy, I know the memory must be painful."

"It is. But I want to tell you."

Colston gave in and took the other chair near Bernadette's bed. Eduardo clasped her soft hand in his as he spoke.

"My wife's mother was mad," he said quietly. "I had no knowledge of it, nor did my grandmother, until the wedding was over. Consuela seemed to be perfectly normal, so I had no reason to suspect things were wrong with her mind. When I brought her here, to the Rancho Escondido, after our wedding in Madrid, the place was falling apart from my long absence during preparations for the ceremony in Spain. I had to work night and day to recoup my losses, to keep from losing the ranch entirely. She was alone too much and it worked on her, especially when she discovered she was pregnant, soon after our arrival." His face tautened as the memories came back. "She hated the idea of the child almost as much as she came to hate me. When he was born, she ignored him totally. I had to find a wet nurse to tend him." He stared down at Bernadette's hand, felt its reassuring grasp. "I fell into debt quite heavily and had to go on a business trip to borrow more money. I tried to get Consuela to come with me, but she wouldn't. She stayed behind with the baby, and I made certain that there would be plenty of servants to watch her and the child, because already I had misgivings about her sanity. When I came home, it was to find her alone in the house. She had dismissed the servants by telling them that she was going to take the baby and join me."

Bernadette's fingers nestled closer against his hand, because she could feel the effort it was taking him to say these things to her father.

He took a long breath. "She was doing needlepoint. She looked at me quite calmly and asked if my trip had been successful. I asked her about the baby, and she looked at me as if she didn't understand what I meant. I went down the hall to the room where the child was kept. It was cold in the house, as it was winter, and a bad one. The fireplace had not been lit at all. The baby was lying in his bed, uncovered. He was emaciated and he had been dead for . . . several days, by the look of him," he added between clenched teeth. "I buried him myself and told no one what had happened. Consuela seemed not to understand when I spoke to her gently about the baby. But that same afternoon, she loaded one of my pistols while I was giving instructions to my men about some things that urgently had to be done on the ranch. She walked up into the mountains behind here, in the freezing cold, without even a shawl." He lowered his eyes to the white bedspread. "She was lying near some rocks when I finally found her, the pistol still clenched in her fingers, stone dead from a bullet to the brain." He lifted his eyes to glance from Bernadette's sympathetic face to her father's. "The servants knew only what I told them, but people will gossip. It was said that she killed the baby and I killed her out of vengeance and tried to make it look like a suicide. That was not true. I knew she had a sickness of the mind. I loved my son, and I mourned him. But I would not have hurt her. She was too frail mentally for the responsibilities of marriage, and none of us knew it until it was too late."

"I'm so sorry," Bernadette said gently. "No wonder you were so upset."

"We knew you didn't hurt her, lad," Colston added in a solemn tone. "I thank you for telling us the truth of it, but you were never the sort to hurt a woman and I knew it." He smiled reassuringly. "The way you fought me over Bernadette only reinforced that attitude. I've been a pretty sorry father, you know. But this girl has a forgiving nature, and I'm learning to live in the present instead of the past."

"We all have to learn that eventually," Eduardo replied. "I want to take Bernadette back home, if she'll go."

"What about those women?" Colston asked warily.

"Oh, I think Bernadette can cope," he murmured dryly.

"I think I can, too," she said. She loved Eduardo desperately, and he was feeling something for her, if only affection. It wasn't much, but it was enough to build on. "Never let it be said that a good Irish girl ran from a fight!"

Colston glowered. "You're as good as anybody and don't you forget it!"

She grinned at him. "I won't."

Eduardo was curious. "Was such a comment made?"

It had been, and by him. Bernadette didn't want to remember what she'd overheard in the hotel after the wedding. "Only an insinuation," she said evasively. "I won't have to pack again," she said, changing the subject. "I didn't have time to unpack."

"I'll bring the carriage back to fetch you," he told her. "And this time," he added firmly, "you'll wear something over your face during the trip to protect your lungs from the dust!"

"Yes, Eduardo," she murmured with a wicked glance.

"Ah, how docile you sound," he said mischievously, "and how well I know that you aren't any such thing."

"You said you were going to be the master in your house," she reminded him. "I was only trying to be suitably subservient."

"You've already shown how humble you are." He glanced amusedly at Colston. "She poured a pitcher of cream over my grandmother."

Colston let out a delighted laugh. "So much for my fears," he said, rising. "I'll get back to work, then. You take care of yourself, lass," he added firmly. "No more carelessness with those lungs. I'm not risking the only daughter I've got!"

Bernadette's face was radiant. She smiled up at her father with pure delight. "I'll be good," she promised.

He winked at her, and went out, leaving her with Eduardo.

They smiled at each other.

"So we begin again," he said softly. "And this time, we won't fall at the first fence."

Chapter Twelve

THE CONDESSA AND LUPE WERE IN THE PARLOR sewing when Eduardo escorted Bernadette back into the house. They looked up, and actually seemed embarrassed.

"Bernadette is still not doing well," he told them formally. "I'm taking her upstairs to lie down until the evening meal."

"Of course," Lupe said, and forced a smile to her lips.

The condessa looked at Bernadette with a subdued expression. "I trust you are feeling better," she said stiffly.

"I'm feeling much better," she replied with deliberate brightness. "Thank you for asking."

Eduardo drew her along with him, nodding politely to his relatives.

The room to which he took her was enormous, with windows that went almost to the ceiling and heavy mahogany furniture. The bed was huge, four-postered, and its cover was a patchwork quilt obviously done by an expert. The curtains were like the chairs, plain and functional rather than pretty. It was a man's room, not a woman's.

"I've slept here since my return to the ranch," he told Bernadette. "You can change the look of it, if you like."

"I won't do anything right away," she told him. She sat down on the edge of the bed, which was so high off the floor that her feet didn't touch the polished wood. She glanced at her husband with a shy smile.

He sighed, leaned against the broad dresser with his arms folded across his chest and studied her. "You look at home on my bed," he said. "I hope you know that I don't mean our marriage to be a platonic one."

"I know."

His black eyes narrowed. "Bernadette, we haven't spoken of a child," he said after a minute. "I know that you have a terror of childbirth. I also know that in the heat of our coming together, I did nothing to try to prevent one."

She was more curious than afraid. "Can you? Prevent a child, I mean? How?"

He chuckled. "More questions!"

"I don't know anything about men and women. Who else can I ask?"

He moved to the bed and sat down beside her. "I can use a sheath," he told her, and explained where and how it was used.

Her eyes widened. "But isn't that uncomfortable for you?"

"A little. And it might be as uncomfortable for you. But it's a tried-and-true method of preventing pregnancy."

She stared down at the tips of her high-button shoes and grimaced.

"Something disturbs you?"

She shifted. "It would be like making love with gloves on," she murmured.

His heart skipped. "I see. And you don't like the idea?"

"I like . . ." She hesitated, not able to look at him. "I like . . . feeling you."

His breathing became audible. "Feeling me . . . inside you?" he whispered.

She caught her own breath. Seconds later, she was on her back on the quilt and Eduardo was making a meal of her mouth. She felt his hands on her body, warm and welcome, and, feeling exquisite hunger, she dragged him down on her.

He hesitated. "One moment."

He got up and locked and bolted the bedroom door. He turned back to her with his hands already working at the buttons of his shirt.

She watched him undress without embarrassment, lying propped on her elbows with her eyes growing larger and larger when he stepped out of the last garment.

He moved toward the bed. She sat up, her

breath coming in gasps. She tore at buttons and fastenings, welcoming his hands when they took over the task.

"Will you have enough breath for this?" he asked tautly as he eased her down on the bed and pulled away the lace-trimmed bloomers she wore.

"Oh, yes," she whispered unsteadily.

He lay her back on the bed and sat beside her, enjoying her nudity. "Take your hair down."

She obliged him, tearing out pins in her haste, because he was obviously going to wait until she finished before he went any further.

He spread her hair over the coverlet, enjoying its soft blond shimmer and its length. He glanced toward the window and noticed that one was open. He got up without a word and went to close it tightly.

He came back to her, solemn and visibly aroused.

"Why did you do that?" she asked as he lay down on the bed beside her.

"You and I make love noisily," he said gently. "I don't want you to hold back your cries for fear of being overheard. I like it when you moan."

She gripped his bare shoulders hungrily as his head bent to her nipples. They peaked at once. He smiled as he suckled them and heard a soft cry break from her lips.

His hands slid under her, around her. One hand slid smoothly down her soft belly and parted her legs so he could enjoy her femininity. She trembled and gasped when he probed and teased her body into eager submission. It arched, pleading for him not to stop.

His mouth slid up to her lips and parted them under its slow, warm pressure.

He took a very long time to arouse her, kindling fires in her body and banking them down. All the while, he smiled at her and kissed her tenderly, watching her helpless reactions and savoring them.

She was so hungry for him that tears stung her eyes. He saw that he couldn't prolong their pleasure unless he did something about her eagerness first. He put his mouth softly over hers and his hand moved on her expertly. She shuddered rhythmically and then stiffened and cried out as he satisfied her.

"Yes," he whispered, lifting his head so that he could see her face. "Is that better?"

She caught her breath on a sob. "Is that . . . all?"

He chuckled. He kissed her wet eyelids. "We've barely begun," he whispered. "But you were far too impatient for what I have in mind. Touch me, Bernadette. I want you to enjoy my body as I intend to enjoy yours." He brought her shy hands to him and taught her what to do with them.

It was like a voyage of discovery. She learned him and he learned her in a breathless, exciting intimacy that made all her inhibitions vanish.

Unlike their first time, he had all the patience in

the world with her. He paused from time to time to calm both of them. Each time he did that, the pleasure escalated to an almost frightening degree. Bernadette had never dreamed that her body was capable of withstanding such a level of physical delight.

She shivered helplessly as the hunger built on itself. Her body was open to him, to his eyes, his hands, his mouth. She lay under him like a creamy sacrifice, her eyes wide open, worshiping the blatant masculinity of him poised just above her.

He was slowly losing his control. He felt himself throbbing and knew that he would have to take her soon if he hoped to satisfy her as well as himself.

He slid his hand over her upper thigh and slowly drew her under him, positioning her with great care and tenderness.

He watched her eyes dilate as he lowered himself on her and began to probe, delicately, that part of her that was eager to accept him. The ease of his passage brought a sharp sigh to his lips. She was so aroused that her body didn't even hesitate as he began to enter her.

She looked down, fascinated with the process of absorbing him. Her hands on his powerful arms contracted with the slow, sweet pleasure.

"So beautiful. So reverent, this joining of male and female, this slow and exquisite loving."

She flinched with a shock of unexpected pleasure when he surged inside her. Her hips arched helplessly, but he caught her thighs and stilled them.

"No," he whispered softly. "It must be slow, amada," he added, moving sensually against her. "It must be very, very . . . slow." His eyes closed and he shuddered with the effort to contain his own impatience. His teeth ground together at the sensations he was beginning to feel. Her body was warm and welcoming, and he felt her contract involuntarily around him and gasped.

She cried out hoarsely, her eyes meeting his in shocked wonder as the depth of his possession surpassed anything that had happened before.

"Can you feel how potent I am?" he asked unsteadily, moving ever closer. "I have never . . . achieved . . . such closeness. . . !!"

She shivered, because the pleasure suddenly became overwhelming, frightening in its explosive impact. "I'm frightened!"

He caught her wrists and forced them to the bed beside her ears. His face was almost menacing, dark and hard as he suddenly pushed down in long, hard, insistent strokes.

"Dear . . . God!" She wept, her face contorting, her body straining as the fierce heat swelled and swelled and swelled.

"Amada," he choked. "¡Mi vida, mi alma, mi corazón . . . !"

His tormented face blurred as she felt the first

contractions ripping through her body. She stilled and convulsed, again and again and again. She couldn't breathe at all. She couldn't feel her heartbeat. She felt the impact of Eduardo's powerful body in waves of exquisite pleasure that was deep enough to be perceived as pain.

She heard her own voice cry out endlessly, as if from a great distance. She whispered something to him, something she barely heard herself, and then she was weeping harshly as the tension snapped and she fell and fell from a great height to land on blazing hot ground.

Eduardo's hoarse groans echoed in her ears as she felt him shudder uncontrollably for what seemed like ages. His hands were bruising her wrists, but even that was sweet. She felt him so deep in her body that she wondered if they hadn't melted together and would become inseparable afterward. Her heart was so full that it overflowed. He had no way of knowing that she had understood the hot, ardent words he'd whispered in Spanish at the height of his pleasure, but she had. He had called her his life, his soul, his heart. He had whispered that she was his loved one. She was as overwhelmed by the confession as she was by the exquisite pleasure they gave to each other.

They held each other in the hot aftermath, sweating and shivering, their hearts racing madly.

Eduardo's sleek, muscular back was damp under her seeking fingers. She felt him deep inside her, and she moved deliberately, because she loved the pleasurable sensations it gave her.

He groaned softly and moved as well. "Bernadette," he said, shaken. He moved again, gasping. "Bernadette, even this close . . . is not close enough."

"Yes, I know." She smiled and her arms tightened around him.

He nuzzled her face with his. "Do you remember what you said to me, just at the last, what you whispered into my ear?"

She did. Her face dived into his throat and pressed there hotly.

"You said, 'Make me pregnant.' " He shivered. "Dear God, I thought I would die after that, trying to get closer. I wanted to penetrate your very soul!"

"Didn't you?" she whispered ardently. "It felt as if you did." Her arms tightened again and she shivered, too. "I want a baby so much," she choked. "I'm not afraid, Eduardo. The doctor in New York said that it wouldn't be dangerous at all. He said I had . . . I had nice, wide hips, and I shouldn't have a hard time." She kissed his throat hungrily, aware of his surprised stillness.

"You really want a child, with me?"

"Oh, yes!"

He turned slowly onto his side, still locked with her, and looked into her soft eyes. His black hair was damp and fell roguishly onto his broad forehead. He touched her swollen mouth carefully.

"The asthma . . . surely that would make it more difficult for you?"

She traced his thick eyebrows and his high cheekbones. "Don't you want a son with me?"

His eyes closed. "Yes," he said tautly. "More than anything in the world!"

She smiled tenderly and reached forward to kiss his hard mouth. She moved experimentally and laughed at the pleasure it invoked. Her gaze met his. "Again," she whispered. "Please."

His hands slid down to her hips and held them against his. He moved sinuously and caught his breath when he felt himself swell.

"Oh . . . yes," she gasped. "Yes!"

He had planned to say something to her, but he couldn't think what it was. His teeth clenched as the fever came upon him again and his hips thrust helplessly against hers.

It was hot and wild and all too quickly over. The tenderness of the time before was eclipsed by the headlong passion they shared. She was as violent as he, biting and clawing this time, a hellcat under his thrusting body. The climax, when it came, lifted them both in a hot flood of satisfaction that left them gasping and spent.

They slept for a long time, sprawled nude on the quilt, in each other's arms. It was dark in the room when they awoke.

Eduardo sat up, groaning as he stretched his

sore muscles. "Señora Ramirez," he murmured dryly, "I think you've sprained my back."

"Are you complaining?" she murmured, rubbing her bare foot over his long leg, insinuating it high up on his thigh.

He caught it and followed it up her body. He found her mouth and kissed her with drowsy passion. "Never," he whispered. "I love the way you are with me in bed, Bernadette. I love the way it feels when we join."

"So do I." She nuzzled her face into his throat. "I'm hungry," she said, like a child.

He chuckled. "I'm hungry, too. Did we eat anything?"

"I couldn't eat breakfast, because I was so sick," she murmured wearily. "I'm starved."

"Shall we get dressed and go in search of food?"

"Yes."

He lit the lamp and studied her with delight as she got out of bed and started dressing. "What an exquisite body you have," he murmured as he retrieved his own clothes from the floor, where they were scattered around the bed. "I never dreamed how sensuous it would be."

"Neither did I," she confided. She paused as she was fastening up her blouse. "Eduardo, am I quite normal?" she asked seriously.

He buttoned his trousers before he caught her by the arms and looked down at her. "Why, because you give yourself so completely?"

"That, and the things I say to you."

He smiled, then bent and kissed her softly. "Bernadette, you're a dream. You're all my hopes fulfilled. I wouldn't change one thing about the way you are with me." He traced her softly swollen mouth tenderly. "The only regret I have, if you could call it that, is my own lack of stamina. I want you far more times than I'm capable of having you."

"Yes, but I never seem to stop," she murmured. "I mean, it happens only one time for you, but I go on and on."

"Women do," he whispered wickedly. "And I love it that you go on and on, because I get as much pleasure from your many times as I get from my one."

"Really?"

He laughed and wrapped her up close. "Really." He sighed. "The first intelligent thing I've done in my life was to marry you."

Her heart jumped. "You truly aren't sorry?"

"No."

"Neither am I."

"You meant it, about a child?" he asked after a minute, drawing back to search her eyes.

"I meant it."

"Then we'll see what happens."

She smiled at him. "Yes."

* * *

They went downstairs together, only to find the parlor deserted. "They've gone to their rooms, I imagine," Eduardo said with a rueful smile. "Probably they felt you needed rest more than conversation."

She looked up at him worriedly. "You don't think they heard us?" she asked.

He smiled. "Our rooms are on the other end of the house. No one heard us."

She wondered if she should confess that she understood what he'd said to her. She searched his dark eyes and decided to wait, just a little longer. She loved him with all her heart. It was paradise itself to know that he shared those feelings. At least, she thought he did. She remembered an old saying, that a man said such things to a woman when he wanted to ensure her cooperation. Perhaps if she were patient, for just a little longer, she might learn what she most wanted to know about his feelings for her.

They settled into a new and consuming togetherness, which was heightened by Lupe's announcement that she was returning to Granada within the week. The condessa was remaining for another few weeks. This news wasn't completely welcomed by Bernadette at first. But when Lupe was gone, the old woman searched out her new granddaughter-in-law in the parlor.

The condessa, leaning heavily on her silver-topped cane, sat down gingerly in a small wing chair across from Bernadette's. Her narrow eyes focused on the intricate stitches the younger woman was putting into the bodice of a new dress she was making.

"You have a flair for this," the condessa said a little stiffly.

Bernadette stared at her. "My grandmother used to visit us occasionally. She taught me to sew, and to crochet."

"I enjoy these occupations as well," came the reply. The condessa shifted in the chair, rustling the black taffeta skirt of her high-necked dress. "Did your mother do handiwork?"

"My mother died at my birth," Bernadette said simply. "I never knew her."

The old woman frowned. "You were an only child?"

Bernadette shook her head. "I had an older sister. She died in childbirth. I have a brother, Albert. He and his wife and son live in Maine."

The condessa stared down at the tips of her shoes peeking out from under her long skirt. She seemed lost in thought. "Childbirth must hold some . . . terror for you, then."

"A little," Bernadette confessed. She looked up from her stitching. "But a physician in New York told me that it would not be especially dangerous for me. I have wide hips, you see, and a strong constitution. Well, except for my lungs," she added with a rueful smile.

The condessa cleared her throat and wiped her lips with a delicately embroidered silk handkerchief clenched in one small hand. "My grandson seems quite capable of dealing with you when your lungs give you trouble."

"He asked Maria, our housekeeper, what to do," she explained. "He was concerned that my father was rather indifferent to my condition." She sighed. "My father has changed a great deal since my marriage to Eduardo. He blamed me for my mother's death for a long time. But he seems very different these days. I think he may even care for me a little."

The condessa looked ruffled. "A child is not responsible for its own birth," she said haughtily. She stared at Bernadette, and it was almost as if the old woman could see the lonely, insecure child she'd once been. The old face softened a little. "My son was my whole world. I raised him and educated him, and permitted him to come here, to inherit this home which my husband's father had built." Her face hardened. "He met that woman in San Antonio, at a fiesta, and dazzled her with his charm and his wealth and his inheritance. They married against my wishes, and for many years we did not even speak." She drew in a slow breath, and the pain of the telling was in the lines in her face. She looked suddenly very old and fragile. "When the news came that he had died, I thought I would die as well." The old woman's lower lip trembled, and tears, great hot tears, rolled down the delicate contours of her wrinkled face.

Bernadette put down her needlework, got to her feet, and sank to her knees at the old woman's side, holding her while she cried.

"I have . . . been tormented," the condessa wept. "I loved my son so!"

"Of course you did."

The condessa wiped her eyes with her handkerchief. "You cannot know the suffering his death caused me."

"I think I have some idea of it." She smiled. "You should talk to God more often," she murmured. "He listens. I talk to Him all the time. I expect He tires of my endless conversation."

The condessa actually smiled. She reached out and touched Bernadette's cheek lightly. "My child, I never expected comfort from you. I have been very unkind." She grimaced. "Eduardo became my life when he was sent home to me as a boy to be raised. I was jealous, and afraid for him when we learned he would marry a rich American woman. I could see history repeating itself and I thought I could not bear it."

"I'm not really rich," Bernadette said. "My father is."

"I think you understand my fears."

"Yes, I do," she replied. "But I could never hurt Eduardo. I love him too much."

"I saw this," the condessa said slowly. "I saw it too late. Can you forgive me for the obstacles I placed in your path?"

"If you can forgive me for pouring cream over you," Bernadette replied, tongue-in-cheek.

The condessa's old face lit up and made her years fall away. "It was an experience I shall never quite forget. And I must say, it was richly deserved. I am glad that I did not cost Eduardo the one bright flower in his life." She shook her head. "He told me about Consuela, finally." Her eyebrows lifted. "You know?"

Bernadette nodded.

"I had no idea. We knew that her mother had some peculiarities, but we had no idea that she was mad, completely mad. Then when Eduardo insisted on taking Consuela to Texas, out of our sight, we knew nothing of his problems with her." She shook her head sadly. "I have so many regrets. One should never meddle in the affairs of others."

"Yes, but sometimes it's very hard not to, when one cares about them."

The condessa smiled. "Yes. It is." The smile widened as she added, "¿Porqué no se dices a mi nieto que puedes hablar español?"

"Porque ahora no es el tiempo para eso."

The condessa laughed. "And why is this not the

time to tell him that you speak his language quite well?"

"Because I learn so much secretly that he wouldn't want me to know," Bernadette said simply. "I'll tell him. Soon."

The condessa searched the sparkling green eyes and thought how nice it would be to have a great-grandchild with such pretty eyes.

Eduardo noticed the improved relationship between the two women in his life with secret amusement. Fences apparently had been mended very quickly, because now in the evenings the condessa sat beside Bernadette while they worked on their various sewing and crocheting projects and they never seemed to run out of subjects to discuss. There was something else between them, too, though, he noticed, because they seemed more and more like coconspirators.

He took Bernadette riding with him one morning when the dew was still on the grass near the house.

She liked to wear old jeans when she rode with him, something that he expected to outrage his very proper grandmother. He was surprised when the condessa chuckled and said that her new granddaughter was a sensible girl not to wear heavy, bulky skirts on horseback.

"You've changed her," Eduardo remarked when they were well away from the house.

"Perhaps she's changed me a little, too. I like her," she added. "She's contrary, of course, and painfully opinionated, but you always know exactly where you stand with her. I shall miss her terribly when she leaves."

"As shall I." He glanced at her amusedly. "I notice that your lamentations don't include Lupe."

Her eyes flashed at him. "I don't miss Lupe," she said curtly. "That flirting, over-perfumed, interfering hussy!"

He threw back his head and roared. "She felt much the same about you, I think."

"She isn't married to you. I am!"

He glanced at her with indulgent affection. "So you are, Señora Ramirez. Very married."

She knew that he was referring to their exquisite nights together, and she blushed in spite of herself.

"Ay, que placer me das. No podia vivir sin ti." What pleasure you give me. I couldn't live without you.

"Nor I, without you," she said without thinking. "Oh, look, Eduardo!"

He was so shocked by her reply to a language he didn't think she spoke that he was diverted immediately. He followed her pointing finger to a small herd of white-tailed deer bounding across their path.

"Beautiful, are they not?" he asked, but his mind was spinning. Did she speak Spanish? And if she did, how much of his private thoughts had he inadvertently given away to her?

"I love it here," she murmured. "And if you notice, my lungs give me less trouble than they ever have before."

"I've noticed." His eyes narrowed as he studied her. "¿Bernadette, es posible que tu me entiendes cuando hablo en espãnol?" Is it possible that you understand me when I speak Spanish?

She glanced at him and put on her most bland expression. "I'm sorry. What did you say?" she asked.

He repeated it, more slowly.

She frowned. "Dear me, you'll have to say it in English. I'm sorry," she said with apparent sincerity. "What did it mean?"

"Nothing," he replied, and seemed to relax. "Nothing at all. Shall we go?"

She urged her mount to keep pace with his and let out a relieved sigh. That was too close a call for comfort!

Chapter Thirteen

CLAUDIA, WHO WORKED IN THE KITCHEN, ARRIVED LATE to fix breakfast, and apologized profusely to Bernadette because she had her two children with her.

She explained in rapid-fire Spanish that her sister was ill and she couldn't leave the little boy and girl, ages three and four, alone with her.

Bernadette chuckled and told Claudia to get on with her chores while she read the children a story.

She proceeded to do that, in flawless Spanish, and was oblivious to the appearance of her husband and his grandmother in the archway that separated the kitchen from the dining room.

Eduardo listened to her as she read and paused to explain some of the harder words, still in Spanish, to the little boy and girl on her lap.

His breath caught. He'd never imagined this . . . and remembered things he'd said in front of her with faint embarrassment, which grew to mammoth proportions when he recalled his uninhibited whispers in bed. And she'd pretended to understand nothing!

His intake of breath was audible. Bernadette's head turned suddenly and she saw in his face that her secret was a secret no longer.

She smiled sheepishly. "Good morning."

"Good morning."

His grandmother chuckled. "So, finally you permit him to share the secret," she said with amusement in her dark eyes. "About time, too! Let the children come into the parlor with me and I will finish the story for them. I believe you two have something to discuss!"

"Something to discuss, indeed!" Eduardo muttered as he closed the bedroom door behind them. He folded his arms and stared at her impatiently.

She went close to him and smiled wickedly as she wreathed her arms around his neck. "A woman has to have some way to find out what her husband really thinks of her," she said. "You never would have told me."

"You think not?" With a long sigh he searched her twinkling eyes. "I wanted you from the first. You must have known."

"I knew that you wanted me," she agreed. "But you could have wanted me without loving me." She hesitated. "I heard everything you said to Lupe and your grandmother about me, Eduardo, just after the wedding. . . ."

"Querida." He groaned, holding her closer. "I would have cut off an arm to spare you that! I wanted you to the point of madness, and then to have them tell me that you'd started scandalous gossip about us . . ." He lifted his head, and his black eyes were apologetic. "Bernadette, my emotions were in such turmoil and I felt at the center of a storm I never thought to weather." He traced her face with tender fingers. "I believe I fell in love with you years ago, but I was afraid of marriage. I had been through so much with Consuela, and the memories of my father's marriage were equally bad. . . ." He bent and kissed her softly. "Can you forgive me?"

"Yes," she said. "I can forgive you."

"From this moment on, I swear to listen to no one except you . . . and my own heart."

She grinned, enjoying his rare apology. "Good! Because I have some very sound advice for you on several matters to do with the bookkeeping around here!"

He chuckled. "Very well. I promise to listen." He sighed softly. "I love you, Bernadette. I don't know when it began, really, but I can't imagine life without you now."

"Nor can I imagine life without you." She turned her head and kissed his warm throat.

"The condessa knew that you spoke Spanish."

She chuckled. "Yes, she did, the wicked old darling, and never said a word to you."

"She has been enjoying her situation lately. She adores you. As I do."

"And I adore her. She was only afraid that you were going to be hurt as your father was. Because she didn't know me, she thought I might be like your mother."

"You could never be like her," he murmured. He drew her closer. "Bernadette, when things are better here financially would you like to travel to Maine and visit your brother?"

"Oh, I'd love to!"

He lifted his head and smiled down at her. "Then it's a bargain." His eyes narrowed. "Our lives aren't going to be easy, for a time. I have done all I can do to pull us back from the edge of bankruptcy, even with the loan your father made me. It may be very difficult."

She reached up her hand and touched his lips. "I don't mind," she said honestly. "We'll do it together."

He nodded. "Together."

It was a long and hard climb back to prosperity. Bernadette proved an amazing asset because of her natural aptitude for bookkeeping and budgeting. She took over the accounts that had been left idle when the stock manager had resigned weeks ago to go back East, and only then did Eduardo begin to see that his latest losses were directly attributable to the man's lack of financial expertise.

"But I had no idea!" he exploded when Bernadette sat him down in the office and began to show him the enormous outlay of cash for supplies, some of which were nothing more than luxuries. "I assumed that he knew what he was doing here." He slapped his forehead and broke into outraged Spanish.

"Now, now," she comforted. "It's not so bad. He wasn't stealing from you, at least, and some of these things are actually in good enough condition to be returned for credit." She bent over the books, rattling off items like saddles and duplicate parts for the new mechanized plow he'd added to his meager store of equipment. "Mr. Jakes at the hardware will take these back and probably be glad to get them, because old man Harrod just bought a mechanized plow himself." She grinned at Eduardo. "He'll be happy to have spare parts."

He shook his head as he looked over her shoulder at the accounts. "You have a natural ability," he marveled. "Amazing!"

"And you thought I was just irresistible physically," she teased with a demure smile.

He touched her hair lightly and then kissed it, just at the temple. "You surprise me constantly. How did I ever manage without you?"

"I have no idea."

He sobered then, as he scanned her penciled figuring on the account book. "We must find other ways to conserve our funds, so that this doesn't happen again." He shook his head. "I could kick myself for trusting the man so completely. I assumed that because he'd managed a ranch before, he knew precisely how to manage the bookkeeping."

"Don't blame yourself. It would escape most people who weren't familiar with the small details of everyday ranch operation." She glanced up at him. "A livestock manager only deals with one aspect, the beasts themselves. Because I had to do all the ordering for our ranch when I was at home, this is something I know very well." She smiled. "My father can scarcely read or write," she confessed. "He's very touchy about having people know it, but it's made life difficult for him in a lot of ways. My mother, I understand, was quite the genius at managing money, and helped him grow rich in their early years together."

Eduardo hugged her. "I can see that my own fortune is assured with her daughter taking care of my ranch for me!"

She chuckled. "It's early yet. But I don't see any reason why we can't pare down these expenses and start making money on cattle, instead of losing it."

After that day, Eduardo came to depend on Bernadette's uncanny financial sense. Her father had to do without it, of course, but Bernadette had found him a good substitute, a former bank clerk who had a way with accounts.

Meanwhile, Eduardo shared his plans and his dreams with her, and when it was time to buy and sell cattle, he made sure that she went with him to the various meetings with other cattlemen. The ranchers were surprised at first when Eduardo insisted that his wife join the discussions. They weren't accustomed to a woman who knew how to evaluate the rise and fall of cattle prices in the market, or the factors involved in successful marketing. But Bernadette made an immediate impression on them when she pointed out some recent news about cattle price fluctuations and the reasons for them. She advised selling off certain stocks and buying others and related her theories for doing it. The ranchers only half listened, convinced that Eduardo was off his head for letting a woman make such decisions.

But when he doubled the price he received for his culled stock, and bought more at a steal, they started listening. Thereafter, when Bernadette advised a strategy for Eduardo, there was an interested audience.

Eduardo found their acceptance of her amusing. "Most of them have wives who sit and sew all day and want to talk about fashion," he confided. "They don't quite know how to deal with a woman who can understand cattle prices."

"I'm enjoying myself."

"Indeed you are," he said solemnly. "Do you realize that we've already doubled our investment in the new strain of Santa Gertrudis cattle we purchased from the King Ranch? They're a hardy breed. Because of their Brahman ancestry, they stand extremes of heat and cold very well, and they have the beef conformation of their Hereford forebears."

"I like their pretty red coats," she told him.

He made a face at her. "I like the prices they bring at auction," he returned. "They gain weight very satisfactorily on the sparse vegetation the land can provide, so we have less need to supplement their feed with expensive grain." He sighed. "Bernadette, for the first time, I have high hopes for our prosperity."

"So do I," she replied. "My father seems to have the same sense of optimism, too. He's glad he made you the loan. And even gladder to have you in the family, I think," she added. "He's always thought highly of you."

"And I of him," he replied. "He may be rough around the edges, but he's a gentleman for all that."

She curled her fingers around the hand resting beside hers on the account book. "We're doing nicely," she said. "But I miss your grandmother."

He kissed her hair. "So do I. She went home only reluctantly, but there were business matters that required her attention."

"She said she'd come back for the first christening," she said, deliberately bringing up a subject that had been taboo between them for most of the four months of their marriage. Despite her fear of childbirth, Bernadette now found herself frustrated and sad that she wasn't pregnant. She was facing the possibility that she might be barren. She knew that the fault couldn't lie with Eduardo, because he and Consuela had produced a son. She felt lacking, somehow. She noticed that Eduardo never talked about their situation, or referred to the fact that four months of marriage had failed to bring about the promise of a child.

He didn't speak for a full minute. His hand absently caressed her pale hair, which was piled into a huge roll around the top of her head. "Perhaps there will be that promise, one day," he murmured.

She looked up at him sadly. "I'm sorry," she said gently. "I know how much you want a son."

He shrugged and forced a smile. "I love you, Bernadette," he said, his voice tender and low. "If a child comes of that love, it will be wonderful, but I can grow old happily even if we live alone together until we die."

"I know," she replied, "but I want a child, too."

He drew her up into his arms and kissed her tenderly. "Don't brood about it," he whispered. "Time will take care of most problems."

"I hope so!"

They went back to the books and delighted in the way the livestock was thriving.

But as with any successful enterprise, trouble was brewing. Eduardo's growing herds were noticed by unscrupulous men home from the Spanish-American War and without means. Several of them banded together and began raiding ranches for beef cattle with which to start their own operation across the border in Mexico.

One night they raided the outlying areas of Eduardo's ranch and made off with over a hundred head of fattened cattle ready to send to market.

Eduardo, when informed of the raid by one of his vaqueros, immediately strapped on his sidearm and loaded his Winchester.

Bernadette almost choked on her fear as he went striding out the door, deaf to her pleas for restraint.

"Take care of her," he said to Claudia as he slammed on his hat. "I'll be back when I can. ¡Muchachos, vámonos!" he called to his men as he swung into the saddle and rode ahead of the well-armed assembly.

He stopped by the Barron ranch and Colston, who had also lost cattle to the rustlers, mounted his own men and fell in with his son-in-law.

Together, they rode down the long trail toward Mexico.

* * *

Filled with anxiety, Bernadette sat at the window and drank endless cups of black coffee so that she could stay awake. Claudia brought her some scrambled eggs and bacon in the early hours of the morning, insisting that she must eat something to keep up her strength.

The strangest thing happened when she lifted a forkful of eggs to her mouth. She stared at them with growing nausea and suddenly jerked up from the table and ran out to the back porch. The endless cups of black coffee made a return appearance. Claudia, rather than being concerned, stood by and clapped her hands and laughed with pure delight.

"I'm sick as a dog, and you can stand there giggling at me?" Bernadette muttered through the spasms that shook her.

"Oh, no, señora, not at the sickness, but at the cause for it. This particular sickness will end in just a few months, and you will have one fine little baby to show for it!"

Bernadette caught her breath. She gaped at Claudia. "Do you think so?"

Claudia nodded, grinning as Bernadette again threw herself over the railing. "Oh, yes," Claudia said. "I think so!"

Chapter Fourteen

BERNADETTE WAS OVERJOYED AND OVERWHELMED AT the prospect of being pregnant, but she was also terrified at the prospect of being a widow even before she could share her hopes with Eduardo.

When the nausea passed, she went back to her vigil at the window and forced herself to pick up her yarn and crochet hook to keep her cold, unsteady hands busy. She thought of the baby and, smiling, began to work on a tiny pair of booties. She could make socks, so these posed no difficulty. The time passed much more rapidly when she was forced to concentrate on what her hands were doing.

She thought about how Eduardo would receive the news about her condition, and she beamed. He would make a wonderful father, and this child might help make up for the loss of his son. She thought of the look he'd have on his face when she told him and her fears died down just a little. But the fear that he might not return was undeniable.

It was well after daylight when she heard the

sound of horses' hooves. She tossed down her crocheting and rushed out to the porch with Claudia at her heels. Her eyes searched wildly for her husband's tall, commanding presence in the saddle. When she didn't see him immediately, it seemed that her worst fears were being realized, and tears stung her eyes.

"Eduardo!" she cried pitifully, her fingers pressing hard against the adobe surface of the house. "He's not there! Claudia, he's been killed . . . !"

"No, no, señora, no!" Claudia exclaimed, rushing to support her mistress's crumpling form. "He is very well, indeed! Look, señora!"

Bernadette followed the smaller woman's pointing finger to Eduardo, well behind the others, riding alongside her father as vaqueros from both ranches herded cattle off toward the nearby fenced enclosures.

"He's all right?" Bernadette's voice sounded hollow to her own ears, and all at once, she went down, despite Claudia's efforts to support her.

Claudia's wildly waving arms caught the attention of Eduardo and Colston, who spurred their mounts and rushed to the porch.

Eduardo was out of the saddle at once. He lifted his unconscious wife, while listening to Claudia's confused explanation of what had happened and carried her into the parlor. He laid her down on the couch, his eyes going with shocked delight to the cast-down crocheting she'd left behind.

"Bernadette!" he called softly, rubbing her hands worriedly. "¡Querida, dígame!"

She heard him as if through a mist. Her green eyes slid open lazily and met his brilliant black ones. She smiled, lifting a hand toward his face, which he grasped and kissed fervently.

"Is she all right? Lass, whatever happened?" Colston Barron exclaimed at his daughter's side.

"It was just relief at seeing Eduardo alive," she whispered. "A child needs both a father and a mother," she added, feeling overwhelming delight.

"A child," Eduardo said, savoring the word. He bent and kissed his wife's pale face with something akin to reverence. "All those worries, for nothing. God is good."

"Oh, yes, He is," she agreed fervently.

"A child," Colston was murmuring. He appeared to be very worried.

Bernadette looked past her husband's exultant face to her father's worried one. "I spoke to a physician in New York," she told her father gently. "He said that I had nothing to fear about childbirth, despite the tragedies in our family. He said that I would be fine!"

Colston still looked perturbed. "You'll take excellent care of yourself, do you hear me? If you need nurses, doctors, I'll make sure you have them, lass."

She smiled happily. "Thank you, Father."

He cleared his throat and looked self-conscious.

"Having a grandchild is an important event," he said. His face began to lighten. "Why, I can teach him all about the railroads, can't I? And about leprechauns and fairies . . ."

Bernadette laughed. "And Eduardo can teach him about his Spanish ancestors," she agreed.

"What a heritage he'll have," Eduardo murmured contentedly, gazing at his wife's waistline with obvious pleasure. "And what a lovely mother."

"Aye, she'll be a perfect one," Colston agreed. "Always around the vaqueros' children at home, she was. She's a natural-born parent."

"I can hardly wait," Bernadette said softly, and meant it.

"Nor can I," Eduardo seconded. But there was faint worry in his face that he was careful to conceal from her.

The ranch went from improvement to improvement over the months that followed. Despite Eduardo's protests, Bernadette continued taking care of the books and accounts, and prosperity followed. There were no more raids on the livestock. The contracted beef cattle were sold, along with a new crop of purebred calves. To Bernadette's amazement, a whole consignment was loaded onto a ship at the coast, bound for Australia.

"I can't believe the sales we're making," she told Eduardo.

"Nor can I." He glanced down at the mound of their child and touched it gently. "How much longer do you think, Bernadette?"

"The doctor says anytime now," she replied.

The muscles in his jaw pulsed.

She pressed as close to him as her huge belly would allow and laid her head against his chest. "Please don't worry. I promise not to die."

He laughed, but it had a hollow sound. He stroked her pale hair gently while his eyes stared blindly into space. She was his life. If he lost her now, neither the ranch nor any other thing on earth would be enough to keep him alive.

"I promise," she repeated, looking up at him. "Eduardo, our lives have been hard until now. Do you really think that God would be so good to us, only to snatch our happiness away just as it begins?"

"You make my fears sound like a sacrilege," he murmured.

"Faith moves mountains," she replied simply. She smiled. "Everything is going to be just fine."

"All right. I'll try not to worry."

But he did, especially when she fell to the floor early one morning in a pool of water and, gasping, called for him to fetch the doctor.

He wouldn't leave her. He sent one of the vaqueros to town, and then to Colston Barron's.

The doctor took forever to come. Meanwhile,

Bernadette was racked with pain and weeping helplessly. Eduardo had no idea what to do. In fact, Claudia quickly shooed him out of the room. When Colston Barron and the doctor arrived, Eduardo was halfway through a bottle of imported Scotch whiskey.

"Fetch me a glass, girl, and make it a large one," Colston told one of the servants. "This is a time for serious drinking."

Eduardo looked at him through bloodshot eyes. "It has been two hours," he said in a choked voice. "I tried to look in the door, and the doctor had one of my own men push me in here." He shrugged. "She screamed," he said through his teeth. "I should have broken down the door to get to her, but she called to me that she would be all right. They are in league against me, she and the doctor." His face darkened as he lifted the glass to his lips again. He looked toward his father-in-law with utter fury. "If she dies, I'll shoot him, right through the eye!"

"She won't die," Colston said with more conviction than he felt.

"I'm going to load my gun."

"Drink your whiskey. You can load your gun later."

Eduardo turned back to the bottle. He studied the glass and then the gun rack. He sat back. "Perhaps it would be wiser to wait. Just briefly."

They drank and talked and worried for another hour. When the doctor came into the room, wiping his hands on a towel, they were laid across chairs in pitiful heaps, both half-coherent and barely able to sit up when he called to them.

The doctor grinned. "Bernadette is fine. It's a boy," he said.

"A boy. A son. Praise God!" Eduardo murmured in a slurred tone.

"Congratulations, my boy, con—"

"—And a girl," the doctor continued.

Eduardo blinked. He wasn't at all sure that he was hearing correctly. "You said a boy," he replied.

"Yes, I did."

"Now you've changed your mind and it's a girl?"

The doctor chuckled. "You're going to have a head the size of San Antonio in the morning. It's a boy *and* a girl," he said. "Twins."

Eduardo's intake of breath filled the room. He grasped the arms of his chair for balance. "Twins!!"

"Twins!" Colston poured himself another drink. "God be praised, twins!"

"Bernadette would like to see you both," he continued. He shook his head as he turned. "God knows why," he added under his breath as they struggled to their feet.

They were far too drunk to have understood him, even if he'd spoken very loudly. With arms around each other for support, they weaved down the dark hall behind the doctor and into the bedroom from which the wails of tiny babies could be clearly heard.

"Good, strong lungs," the doctor murmured as Claudia came forward with both infants in her arms. "And I can include your wife in that. Her asthma didn't surface once during the whole long labor." He grinned. "I think I may write a paper on her."

"Que guapos son," she expressed with a radiant smile as she showed her small charges to Eduardo. "They are so beautiful, señor."

"Beautiful," he pronounced, touching each tiny face reverently. "Like my Bernadette."

He moved toward the bed, leaving Colston to admire his grandchildren, and sat down next to a weary, worn Bernadette, who still somehow managed to smile and lift a hand to pull him down to her.

She kissed him softly. "We have children," she whispered weakly. "A son and a daughter."

"And you are alive, as you promised me, and with lungs that didn't even hinder you through this entire ordeal," he said. He kissed her again. "Bernie, I'm very drunk."

She laughed at the unfamiliar nickname he'd just given her. "Very drunk, indeed!" she scolded. "Didn't you trust me?"

"I tried to," he said. "But trust is hard when people scream, you know." His radiant eyes met hers. "I love you more than my life," he whispered tenderly. "Thank you for being alive. And thank you most especially for our children."

She nuzzled her face into his shoulder. "Thank you, too."

He glanced toward his father-in-law, who had taken a chair and was holding one of the babies, crooning softly to it. Bernadette lifted her face and followed his fascinated gaze. Tears stung her eyes at the sight of her father with his grandchild.

"Do you believe in miracles, Eduardo?" she asked, thinking of how distant she and her father had once been, and how chaotic her life had been just the year before. So much had changed. She couldn't have imagined such happiness.

"Yes," Eduardo answered the soft question. But he was looking at her.

She smiled up at him. They had a prosperous cattle ranch, two new babies, and the whole world with its arms open to them. She wondered if she were dreaming it all.

"Darling, would you like to pinch me, just in case?" she asked him.

He chuckled, because he knew what she meant. "Only if you agree to pinch me in return." He leaned closer. "But perhaps we won't take the chance, dearest. If I am dreaming, let me never wake!"

Bernadette couldn't argue with that sentiment. She smiled and kissed him instead, to the soft whisper of an Irish lullaby that came lovingly, but sadly out of tune, from the general direction of the window seat. She thought that she'd never heard such a beautiful song in her life.

Beloved author Susan Carroll took the romance world by storm with her captivating novel
THE BRIDE FINDER

Now read her irresistible, utterly gripping tale of passion and defiance . . .

WINTERBOURNE
By Susan Carroll

"[An] enchanting love story . . . A real treasure."
—*Affaire de Coeur*

In the harsh, turbulent Middle Ages, lovely Lady Melyssan remains as she always has been—sweet, timid and content to be alone. But in a desperate move to resist the advances of the dreaded king, she claims to be married to his worst enemy, Lord Jaufre de Macy, the legendary Dark Knight.

Seeking temporary shelter in Jaufre's abandoned castle, Winterbourne, she is unprepared for the fierce, angry warrior who returns to confront her. But neither Jaufre's dark heart nor Melyssan's innocent one can resist the love that is their destiny—nor protect them from the danger drawing near. . . .

On sale November 3

LOOK FOR THESE TWO DELIGHTFUL REGENCY ROMANCES

MARRY IN HASTE

By Lynn Kerstan

While trespassing on a lavish estate, Diana Whitney strikes Colonel Alex Valliant squarely on the head with a frying pan. Rather than see the pretty interloper fall into disgrace, the love-struck soldier asks for her hand. But Diana refuses to march quietly to the altar and—much to the colonel's surprise and dismay—rejects his offer.

But when Diana's uncle threatens to marry her off to a man she finds completely intolerable, she accepts Alex's hasty proposal. However, Diana soon must make a bold gamble based on the calling of her heart—and engage in a battle for a future founded on love. . . .

THE HOMECOMING

By Marion Chesney

In this final volume to the ever-popular Daughters of Mannerling series, the Beverley sisters have one last chance to regain their ancestral home: Lizzie, the precocious, youngest sister, who would rather die an old maid than marry for anything but love.

And how could she ever love Mannerling's new owner the stuffy Duke of Severnshire? Suddenly, it appears that no one, including the duke, is what he or she seems, and for the first time, saucy and canny Lizzie is at a loss for words. But is a homecoming really what she wants?

ON SALE NOW